DANCE WITH SNAKES

Biblioasis International Translation Series

General Editor: Stephen Henighan

I Wrote Stone: The Selected Poetry of Ryszard Kapuściński (Poland)
    Translated by Diana Kuprel and Marek Kusiba

Good Morning Comrades by Ondjaki (Angola)
    Translated by Stephen Henighan

Kahn & Engelmann by Hans Eichner (Austria-Canada)
    Translated by Jean M. Snook

Dance With Snakes by Horacio Castellanos Moya (El Salvador)
    Translated by Lee Paula Springer

DANCE WITH SNAKES

Horacio Castellanos Moya

DANCE WITH SNAKES

TRANSLATED FROM THE SPANISH
BY LEE PAULA SPRINGER

BIBLIOASIS

Originally published as *Baile con serpientes*, El Salvador, 1996.
© Horacio Castellanos Moya, 2001, first published by Tusquets
Editores 2002. By arrangement with Literarische Agentur Mertin
Inh. Nicole Witt e. K., Frankfurt am Main, Germany.

FIRST EDITION

Library and Archives Canada Cataloguing in Publication

Castellanos Moya, Horacio, 1957-
      Dance with snakes / Horacio Castellanos Moya ; translated
from the Spanish by Lee Paula Springer.

Translation of: Baile con serpenties.
ISBN 978-1-897231-61-6

      I. Springer, Lee Paula   II. Title.

PQ7539.2.C34B3413 2009   863'.64   C2009-904018-2

Cover Image: Muybridge Animal Locomotion, plate 73, c. 1887,
Eadweard Muybridge photographer, Collections of the University
of Pennsylvania Archives.

Edited by Stephen Henighan

PRINTED AND BOUND IN CANADA

The old man scratched his chin. Snakes are like people, he said. You have to get to know them. Then you can be their friends.

Allal hesitated before he asked: Do you ever let them out?

—Paul Bowles: "Allal"

ONE

None of the tenants could say exactly when the yellow Chevrolet had first parked in front of the building. There were too many cars that spent the night on that street, a double row that ran the length of the housing project's four blocks. But the yellow Chevrolet attracted attention for a number of reasons. It was a heap that looked at least thirty years old, with a smashed-up body and windows boarded up with pieces of cardboard. It looked like an old wreck that a neighbour wouldn't take to the scrapyard for sentimental reasons.

The first to notice that there was something strange about the car were the housewives and maids who went out in the mornings to go shopping or just to gossip. At that time, a ragged man with grey hair and a beard would emerge from the Chevrolet, looking like someone who'd just woken up after spending the night in his wreck.

Niña Beatriz, who ran the store, made it her business to keep tabs on this strange person and to tell the neighbours about his activities. It was through her that we learned of his daily routine. He'd leave the car at ten in the morning, wander off to some unknown part of the city and somewhere between eight and ten at night, he'd come back carrying a canvas bag full of trash and shut himself up in the car until the next day.

I was the ideal neighbour to snoop on this individual. Unemployed and without any real hope of finding a decent job in these new and troubled times, I was living in the apartment of my younger sister Adriana and her husband Damián. Every month, as a symbolic gesture, I gave them some of the money sent to me from the United States by my older sister Manuela, the one who'd raised me, the one who loved me the most. My situation was very difficult – my degree in sociology (a major no longer offered by most universities) wasn't helping me find a job, as there were too many teachers around, companies didn't need sociologists, and a career in politics – the only other field in which I could have applied my knowledge – was a profession alien to my abilities.

I spent most of my time in the apartment, watching television and reading the newspaper. (I still hoped that one day, I'd find the classified ad that would change the course of my life.) I also helped Adriana run errands and, once in a while, when the opportunity presented itself, I would go see one of those solemn types who, after looking at my résumé, would ask me to give them a call – a call that was never answered.

I first met the man in the yellow Chevrolet on my way to the store for some cigarettes. He was getting out of the car, holding his canvas bag. He wore jeans that had once been blue, grubby running shoes laced up with string, and a tattered T-shirt. His belt looked like a snake. I politely said hello. He didn't answer. Instead, he shut the car door and limped down the street, sullen and reeking of alcohol and urine.

"He's a disgusting drunk," said Niña Beatriz, a plump older woman with a sharp tongue, while she looked for a pack of cigarettes. "He doesn't talk to anyone. Who knows how he ended up here. We should do something to get rid of him."

I talked about him with my sister and brother-in-law at dinner. He didn't look like an ordinary beggar, but seemed to have once been a middle class sort of person. I thought the Chevrolet might really belong to him. My brother-in-law had never seen him, but he had seen the car and wondered whether it still worked.

"He got here somehow," Adriana said, "it's been here less than two weeks." When I told them about the snake around his waist, I was met with their usual unbelieving stares.

A few days later I ran into him again, this time at night, when he was coming back to the car with his canvas bag loaded with what I assumed was trash. I caught up to him, said, "Good evening," and started to walk beside him. "I'm Eduardo Sosa, your neighbour," I said. He didn't turn around to look at me, but kept walking, as though I'd never spoken to him, as though I weren't even standing next to him. I continued: "Living in a car must be pretty uncomfortable." He gave off the same rancid stink and he was moving his lips, muttering to himself. I kept walking beside him. I'd already had a coffee, there wasn't a movie worth watching on TV that night, and he'd piqued my curiosity. He wasn't wearing the snake-belt. "The neighbours are complaining about you. They're going to call the authorities to come and take you away."

He was less than sociable. He looked at me with contempt and blurted, "What's it to you? Why are you sticking your nose in? Go away. Leave me alone."

We got to the yellow Chevrolet. He rummaged through his bags, took out a key and before opening the door, angrily turned to face me. Through clenched, filthy teeth he asked, "What do you want?"

"To see what's inside that car," I said without hesitation. Bewildered, and almost fearful, he turned his back to me, opened the Chevrolet's door and quickly got inside. I couldn't make out a thing. I knocked on the side windows and the windshield, but sheltered behind the cardboard, he didn't answer. I went to the store.

"We've got to call the authorities to come and get rid of that filth," I told Niña Beatriz. She agreed. "Why don't you call the police and get them to send somebody," I suggested. She looked doubtful. I warned her that having someone like that parked in front of her store was bad for business. We should act right away. Otherwise, he'd never leave.

The police car arrived about ten minutes later.

"This Chevrolet has been parked here for about two weeks," said Niña Beatriz. "And a suspicious-looking man is sleeping inside."

"So what's the problem?" asked the police officer, who'd said his name was Dolores Cuéllar.

"What do you mean, what's the problem?" she cried. "We don't know if the car is stolen. The guy is living on the street. And he's a beggar. Understand?"

Two neighbours who had just come into the store agreed with Niña Beatriz. I stayed discreetly in the background. Officer Cuéllar seemed to understand. He walked up to the Chevrolet, knocked on the driver's side window, identified himself as a police officer and demanded that he open the door. There was no answer from inside. By now, half a dozen onlookers surrounded the car.

"He's there. He just got in. This man's a witness," said Niña Beatriz, pointing at me. The officer tried again, this time harder, as though his next step would be to smash the window.

The man stepped out of the car. But instead of being intimidated by the sight of so many people, especially a policeman, he was aggressive, like a caged animal. He said his name was Jacinto Bustillo, that the car belonged to him and, as proof, he showed the officer his car's registration papers. He said he didn't understand why we were bothering him. Parking on the street wasn't illegal.

"Parking here isn't, but you're living in there," Niña Beatriz said, pointing at the car. "And that isn't normal. It's against the law and decent people don't do it. You can't live in the road."

"Why not?" he asked defiantly. "There's no law that says I can't live in my car. Do you know of any law that says I can't be here?" he asked a surprised Officer Cuéllar.

"Well, honestly, no, I don't," stammered the policeman.

He got back in his car.

We stood frozen, not knowing what to say, looking at one another. The officer was the first to leave, saying there was nothing more he could do.

"How can this be!" cried Niña Beatriz, as I walked her to the store.

"I think we were going about this the wrong way," I said. "We shouldn't have called the police. They aren't responsible for this kind of thing. We should go down to City Hall."

She promised to call the municipal authorities first thing the next day. That Jacinto Bustillo wasn't going to get his way. Tomorrow morning he and his filth would have to go someplace else. I started back to the apartment. When I got to the Chevrolet, I knocked on the driver's side window again. "Don Jacinto," I called, "would you like a cigarette?" He didn't answer. I knocked again and repeated the offer.

"Get out of here! Leave me alone!" he yelled, without even poking his head out the window.

I shut myself up in my room to watch TV and enjoy a smoke. I cleaned the dirt out from under my nails with my old pocketknife, the one with the bone-coloured handle.

Next morning, Niña Beatriz told me she'd phoned City Hall, but they'd told her it would take days to send the inspectors over because they were swamped with work. Back in the apartment, I leafed through the newspaper. At a quarter to ten, I went down to the Chevrolet to smoke a cigarette and enjoy the morning sun. He got out, right on time, with his empty canvas bag, looking furious, either because he'd seen me or because that was just the way he was. "Good morning, Don Jacinto," I greeted him brightly, the way you would the most well-liked person in the neighbourhood. He limped past, glaring at me, annoyed. He still reeked of alcohol and stale urine. As usual, I had the whole day ahead of me and nothing to do. "I admire you for what you said to the police last night," I said. "It's important to have some character, to not let other people intimidate you. Of course, I'd already warned you they were coming." I was walking beside him, talking with my hands, happy to be in his company. He stopped.

He stared right into my eyes, and with all the anger he could muster he said, "I'd like to ask you a favour. Leave me alone. Just go away." He didn't speak, he spat the words out.

"Don't worry, Don Jacinto," I said. "I haven't got anything else to do. Relax. I'll go along with you." He started walking again, as if it were possible to ignore me. "I bet you follow the same routine every day," I continued. We were heading downtown. He walked at a steady pace, without stopping, his gaze fixed on the ground. "Tell me about your life, Don Jacinto." But there was no way to break his silence. Maybe he was waiting for me to get tired of this, to give up and trudge back to my sister's apartment. But I was wound up. I told him about my two sisters, about my parents who'd died before their time, about my unemployment, and about the feelings of loathing that sometimes came over me. I think that was how I managed slowly to soften him up. Under an increasingly hot sun, we walked towards the industrial part of the city. It was an area I was unfamiliar with, where asbestos-roofed sheds housed hundreds of women who slaved under the whip of cruel, dirty Chinamen; at least that's what the newspapers said. It was the perfect setting for Don Jacinto to begin telling me his story, the very excrescence I'd been sniffing out – a sewer of garbage, the remains not of the infamous sweatshops that surrounded us, but of a life so ruined that all that remained of it was the wretch by my side and his yellow Chevrolet.

"An accountant? You? I never would have guessed," I exclaimed, brimming with curiosity. I was happy that he was finally confiding in me. The sun was nearly unbearable now and I couldn't get used to the sight of the sweaty old man poking through the dumps near the stream than ran behind most of the factories. He swigged from a bottle of rum that he stubbornly refused to share, distrustful as ever.

I watched him pick up useless junk and throw it into his canvas bag. As though with a picklock, I pried open the story of a man who years ago had been chief accountant of one of the factories we were walking behind. A man who'd been fired suddenly with a generous settlement, but who was nonetheless completely destroyed, not so much because he'd never find another job, or because of the psychological impact of his sudden dismissal, as though the life he'd given to the company had been worthless, but because without a job, he found himself trapped in a miserable home with a repulsive wife and an adolescent daughter who was just like her mother.

"It was revolting, young man, just revolting," he mumbled after we'd wolfed down sandwiches on a street corner under the midday sun, surrounded by workers changing shifts. He took another swig from his bottle of rum. I lit another cigarette.

The whole time we were walking he'd ask me over and over again what my intentions were, what I was looking for, why I wanted to follow him, to find out about his life. I must be up to something fishy, he said, to be wasting my time like this. But he had nothing to lose now, nothing mattered anymore, not even the yellow Chevrolet. He bought the old heap when he'd decided to give it all up and dedicate himself to mere survival. With nothing but his car, he slept in different parts of the city, far from the filth that the rest of us called family, success, work. In a charming yet evasive way, I answered that I was just curious, I wanted to see the world in a different way. It had nothing to do with sociology or field work. It was more like a premonition that somehow my life had something to do with his wandering.

We left the industrial area and walked to streets crammed with pawnshops, where the foul-smelling man who said his name was Jacinto Bustillo opened his canvas bag to show off his precious junk and was welcomed like a valued customer. I stayed out of the way on the sidewalk, smoking, like a bodyguard hidden behind the crowd of transients. I kept a careful eye on Don Jacinto's dealings. Every once in a while, he'd take out his bottle of rum and, without allowing the other party to make even the slightest objection, he'd propose a toast. His partner would then raise his own flask, and the deal was sealed.

Admiring him, I said, "You're a master businessman, Don Jacinto." He smiled reluctantly and stroked his grey beard.

It was well into the evening and his canvas bag was still full of trash. Each of his transactions took enormous amounts of time, trial and effort. We headed to the red-light district, where sordid, putrid flesh seeped from every seedy hole-in-the-wall.

"Looking for any bar in particular?" I asked. His bottle of rum was nearly empty.

"It's called Prosperity," he said.

We walked inside. It was murky, fetid, with saw-dust-covered floors and a couple of rickety tables. The tiny, filthy bar sold only hard liquor.

"So the old dirtbag has company tonight," said a mocking voice at the back. Don Jacinto went up to the bar to have his bottle filled and then straight over to the wretch who'd made the remark, a bald, toothless dwarf with almond-shaped eyes called Coco. Don Jacinto offered me his bottle for the first time. I took a long, hard swallow, enough to set my guts on fire in a single shot, and the burning started right away.

"And who's this gorgeous creature?" Coco asked lustily.

"A curious little shit who hasn't left me alone all day," Don Jacinto said, passing me the bottle again. I took another swig, this time with more conviction. "Who knows what he's up to."

"A little angel from heaven," said Coco, with a perverted sneer. A hateful smile played at the corner of his mouth. I took the bottle from Don Jacinto again, while he insisted that I was a regular piece of shit who'd conspired with a bunch of vile old women last night to get the police to take him away.

"On the contrary," I explained, "I went to warn you about Niña Beatriz's intentions. Don't be ungrateful."

"Now you're going to tell us the truth," Coco said.

"He wants to know why I lead this kind of life."

Coco let out a guffaw. He wanted to look sinister, that fucking dwarf, so he could make a good impression on Don Jacinto, but the old man wouldn't stop passing me his bottle. Then, suddenly, glassy-eyed, he said we should get out of this dump and get a refill. He went back to the bar, got his bottle filled and went outside, followed closely by Coco and me, the unemployed sociologist. I was starting to get dizzy walking along the dark and winding streets with this pair of miserable indigents who shared nits as well as hiding places, like the laneway we found ourselves in now. We sat down outside to have a drink with our asses on the stairs and our backs against a foul-smelling wall.

"I'm going to taste that meat," mumbled Coco, rubbing his hands together. I thought the mangy dwarf was coming on to me, but instead, he lunged toward Don Jacinto's fly. Don Jacinto let him do it, sipping at his bottle, breathing more and more heavily while that bald queen quickened his pace. All of a sudden, Don Jacinto let out a yell and Coco rolled onto the ground, laughing.

"You bit me, you son of a bitch!" he howled. Then, with one swift movement, he smashed the bottle into Coco's face. "You goddammed bastard!" He stuck the broken end of the bottle over and over again into Coco's belly, while he covered his bloody member with his other hand. Coco wasn't even struggling now. He was a bloody mess, his face a hideous grimace and his guts spilling out on the ground. I got up, afraid that Don Jacinto would turn on me, but he sat back on the stairs, exhausted, and moaning over the spilled rum. He swore at Coco's body and told me to go to the store to get more liquor. He was looking through his canvas bag for an empty bottle when I took out my pocketknife, the one with the bone-coloured handle, and slit his throat. His eyes were open in shock above his grey beard. I rifled through his pockets until I found the key to the yellow Chevrolet, picked up the canvas bag and headed back. I crossed the city as fast as I could, anxious to get back to the car, to uncover the private life Don Jacinto had guarded so jealously. I was smart enough to stop off and buy some candles to light up what I sensed would be a dark cavern full of booby traps. I got there just as Niña Beatriz was closing her store. The group of neighbours who collected there and on the corner had already cleared out. I headed straight for the yellow Chevrolet, opened the door and climbed into the dark interior.

The stink nearly knocked me out. I lit a match, a cigarette and a candle. I found a flashlight next to me and turned it on. The place was extremely tidy. There were no seats except for a single stool. It reminded me of a ship's cabin. Rows of bottles and cans formed a kind of control panel. There were blankets piled up in the corner. An overwhelming feeling of happiness came over me. This was my space; from now on, it belonged only to me. I lay down on a blanket, turned off the flashlight and smoked. Tomorrow I'd have time to look the place over carefully. I was exhausted and needed to rest.

Then, just as I put out my cigarette and settled into a fitful sleep, I felt something slippery sliding slowly, revoltingly, against my body. I was paralyzed with fear. There was no doubt. They were snakes. What kind of snakes, I couldn't tell. Snakes that had been hiding in the darkest corners of the car. I stayed still, trying to calm my beating heart, to clear my mind, to not let myself be carried away by my extreme terror. I could make out at least six ophidians slithering over my chest and between my legs. One of them moved across my neck and under my left ear. I tried to control my breathing. Of course – these were Don Jacinto's pets, replacements for the wife and daughter who'd scorned him. If I could manage to keep myself under control for just a few more minutes, if I could concentrate enough so they'd feel my vibrations and understand that I was the new Don Jacinto, I'd be saved, and the greatest scare of my life would be transformed into the kind of greeting that a group of pets gives its new master. It worked. I stayed still for about five minutes, feeling as if I were Don Jacinto, as if the pocketknife with the bone-coloured handle were a kind of scalpel I'd used to make an enormous incision that allowed me to penetrate the world in which I wanted to live. The snakes slowly left my body, but I didn't move until I was sure that my life would continue just the way I'd pictured it. Then I sat up, lit a match and looked for the flashlight. The damned things were there, each one in its place, coiled up and watching me. I lit a cigarette. I started to whisper, to tell them that the filthy old man had been transformed into the person who was now speaking to them. Of course, they understood me. I could see it in their tiny eyes; in the way they moved their tongues when I spoke to them directly. I told myself I needed to name them and learn how to recognize each one. I wondered how the hell Don Jacinto had managed to obtain and tame the snakes. The one next to the stool could be called Beatriz, like the shopkeeper, they clearly had something in common. But this late at night, and being so tired, I couldn't say exactly what. Now that I knew I was captain of this cabin and master of this fearsome crew, I could relax the way I deserved to, at least until the morning, when I'd know for sure that this hadn't been a dream, but the real thing.

Next day when I opened my eyes, I was afraid that I would find myself in my room in Adriana's apartment and see that the whole thing had been a feverish hallucination. But what I saw was the yellow Chevrolet's rusty ceiling. Before I even moved, I remembered Beatriz's deadly eyes and her slippery sliding along my neck. After a while I sat up. They weren't anywhere to be seen.

Clearly, they liked the night. I didn't snoop around. I knew they were there somewhere and that they'd come out when they felt like it, insolent, and obeying only what I'd inherited from Don Jacinto. As soon as I got comfortable, I took the cardboard off the windshield, put the key in the ignition and kept turning until I heard the reluctant cough of the motor. I moved the little stool in front of the steering wheel. I lit my morning cigarette and told myself that Niña Beatriz would have a pleasant day thanks to my efforts and my desire to move the vessel that Don Jacinto had left adrift. And off we went, at full speed, the yellow Chevrolet, the snakes and I, happy and anxious to get to other parts of the city, where we would begin the adventure of our new lives.

I made my way to the largest shopping mall in the city, where I hoped the yellow Chevrolet wouldn't be noticed in the vast parking lot. I parked right in the middle of the lot, surrounded by other cars, so the security guards would have no reason to bother us. I covered the windshield with the cardboard again, turned on the flashlight, and took a bundle of papers out of the glove compartment. I wanted to uncover all the details of Don Jacinto's life. I found his licence, his registration, some old receipts, a beat-up address book, a pile of letters and a couple of newspaper clippings. He was barely forty-two years old, his wife's house was located in a well-off suburb, and the letters had been sent by someone called Aurora, who seemed to have been his lover. I got ready to study these missives with inquisitive delight, when I noticed some movement in the corner of the car. They all appeared at the same time, slithering towards me. They didn't move aggressively. In fact, I'd say it was with caution. There were only four of them, not half a dozen, as I'd thought the night before. Now that I could see the way they each looked more clearly, I was able to name them once and for all. The plump one with the cunning eyes would be Beti; the slender one who moved timidly, almost delicately, would be Loli; Valentina exuded sexuality with her iridescent skin; and little Carmela had an air of mystery about her.

"Good morning, ladies," I said. I lay down on a blanket to keep reading the letters and, to my great delight, I found Don Jacinto's supply of rum next to me. I drank from a bottle, lit another cigarette and started to read. It was a typical tale of romance between a chief accountant and his secretary, both married, he, middle-aged, and she, in the prime of her youth. "It couldn't have been just a soap opera story. Something more profound, more devastating must have happened to poor Don Jacinto," I said to Beti.

She raised her flat head, narrowed her eyes even further, and wagged her forked tongue. "They killed her."

"What!" I exclaimed, surprised that they already knew the whole story.

"Her husband killed her when he found out she was cheating on him with Don Jacinto," she explained.

I took another long swig from the bottle. I put the letters and the other documents back in the glove compartment. It would be better if the ladies told me Don Jacinto's story.

"He had her killed," Valentina clarified, without moving. She was stretched out from under the steering wheel all the way to the back of the car.

Suddenly I realized that I was covered in sweat. Judging by the sweltering heat, it might have been noon already.

"He never told us the details," Beti said. "He'd only say that the husband had her killed in a staged robbery."

So that was the burden that Don Jacinto had been carrying, I thought.

"But that wasn't all," Loli murmured indignantly, without uncurling herself. "The husband told Don Jacinto's wife and daughter the whole story, including the murder, to make sure he really destroyed him."

That was when I heard the sound of someone circling the car, banging on the body, asking where the old heap had come from. I slipped a piece of the cardboard back from the driver's side window. It was a pair of security guards from the mall. What a nuisance. The best thing would be to wait until they got tired of being out in the sun and went to eat. Carmela tensed. She was upright and started to hiss.

"Relax," I whispered, "they're going to leave."

But they weren't leaving. They were talking about calling a tow truck to take the car out of the parking lot. A piece of junk like this went against the shopping mall's regulations, and if one of the bosses caught them doing nothing about it, they'd be reprimanded.

I got out of the car.

Surprised, they looked at me with a distrust that quickly turned to hostility. They ordered me to leave the parking lot immediately – this was private property, not a homeless shelter. I told them that I was just going to the supermarket to buy a bottle of water, but they said I was in no condition to walk down the aisles. What would decent people say? Hadn't I noticed what I looked like? Couldn't I smell the stink? They stood in front of me with their hands on their clubs, determined not to let me pass, to force me to leave. But I'd carelessly left the car door open. And the ladies couldn't stand it. That was why Don Jacinto had always closed it so quickly when he got out of the car.

The security guards weren't so composed once they saw that Beti had got out and was slithering towards them, hissing, her flat head raised, her eyes deadlier than ever. Terrified, they took off like a shot. But Carmela had a different nature; she was barely out of the car when she threw herself in the air and wrapped her body around one of guards' neck. He couldn't even defend himself. The impact and the pressure on his windpipe killed him instantly.

"That's enough," I said, so they'd get back in the car.

But Valentina said they'd come with me to get water; it had been a long time since they'd been out for a stroll and they were sick of being cooped up in the car. I told them to be discreet and try not to make a racket. It'd be best if they followed underneath the cars while I looked for a faucet to fill up the bottles. Then they should go back to the Chevrolet. But there wasn't a tap anywhere in that vast expanse of pavement, at least not one that I could find, so I decided to go to the supermarket. I went into the mall and, to my great surprise, I saw that the four of them were right behind me, smugly following me down the corridor in single file. This caused quite a fuss. Terrified people ran screaming into the stores. There was no turning back now. I was dying of thirst and I had to get to the supermarket. The problem was that all the commotion was affecting the ladies, especially Loli, the shy one. She hurled herself onto an elegant woman who was coming out of a small and very exclusive boutique, unaware of the disturbance, and bit her on the calf. Stiff with fear, the woman shrieked and fell to the ground, convulsing and foaming at the mouth until she turned purple and was still.

The mall was suddenly empty, and we turned and filed into the entrance of the supermarket. I ran, because a security guard was hurrying to close the glass doors, but Beti was quicker and threw herself onto his wrist. He rolled around on the ground, howling. He tried to pull out his gun but was overcome with violent shaking. He banged his head twice on the ground and stayed down. The frightened customers were running towards the back of the grocery store. Valentina slid majestically over to them. I drank a bottle of water, then grabbed another and went to get cigarettes, loaves of bread, and some cans of tuna and sardines. Before I walked over to the exit, I spotted Valentina crushing the neck of a young guy who looked like a gang member. Back in the mall, the alarms wailed and I moved quickly, aware that the police would arrive any minute. A security guard at a jewellery store managed to open the plate glass door halfway. He took a shot in my direction, but in that instant, the ladies caught up with me and, furious, they turned to face him. We rushed to the Chevrolet. I took the cardboard from the windshield, sat on the stool, started the car and headed for the exit.

I drove calmly. I even removed the cardboard from the driver's side window and opened it so we could get a little air. The four of them were looking at me, surprised. Beti said they'd never seen so much excitement in so little time. I smiled, pleased to see them happy. I reached for the bottle of rum and took a big swallow. I lit a cigarette. Then I realized that I was driving towards the suburb where Don Jacinto's wife surely still lived. I opened the glove compartment, took out the registration and read the exact address. It was easy to find the house. I parked in front and covered the windshield and window again. I was about to get out, when Beti stopped me.

"You aren't just going to leave us here, are you?"

I told her that if I showed up with the likes of them, Don Jacinto's wife would die of fright and then I wouldn't be able to tell her what had become of the old man.

Loli muttered that it wasn't fair to leave them shut up in the car; they'd known Don Jacinto longer than I had and they wanted to meet his wife and daughter. Carmela agreed and Valentina shot me a pleading look. I told them I would take them on condition that they stay hidden and not let themselves be seen by anyone in the house. They agreed. I opened the car door and they got out. I lost sight of them.

I rang the bell. From behind the door, a woman's voice asked me who I was. I said I had an urgent message from Don Jacinto Bustillo. She opened the door partway, without undoing the chain. She looked at me with displeasure and then noticed the yellow Chevrolet.

"What do you want?" she asked.

I repeated that I had a message from Don Jacinto for his wife. She told me that he'd disappeared, that he might be dead, that he had no wife now. Although she was looking at me with disdain, I could tell that she was the one I'd been looking for.

"He hasn't died," I said. "He's in hospital and he asked me to talk to you. They're going to operate on him, he's got terrible cancer and he may not survive. He gave me a bank account number and told me the steps you need to follow so that if he does die, they can give you and your daughter the money."

She seemed surprised and looked at the Chevrolet again.

"Doña Sofía, right?" I asked, remembering the name I'd read hastily in one of the letters.

"I don't understand," she said, as though already counting in her head. "What hospital is Jacinto in?"

"In the one run by the Red Cross," I said, "in the emergency room." She finally undid the chain. I walked into a large room with rugs, paintings on the walls, and a small table crowded with family photographs.

"How do you know Jacinto?" she asked stiffly, without offering me a seat.

"It's a long story," I said. "I'm his friend. He told me about the tragedy, the events that drove him from this house. Where is your daughter?"

"At school."

I wondered whether the ladies had managed to get into the house and where they might be hiding. I went over to the table with the pictures, but I didn't see any of Don Jacinto.

"I still can't believe it," she said. "You'll have to explain this bank account thing to me again."

I began to despair. I needed a drink; I needed to be away from this place, far from this insidious woman. I asked her to get some paper and a pencil so I could give her the instructions. When she turned around, I took out my pocketknife and pounced. She dodged me, and struggled and screamed but I caught her with my arm. I thrust the knife deep into her stomach. I stabbed her until she went down, her mouth and eyes open. Her nails loosened from my arm. A young maid appeared in the hallway. She stopped when she saw my knife and my blood-spattered clothes. But I didn't need to act – the four snakes attacked her as one. The poor thing crumbled and convulsed a few times before swelling up so badly that she looked like she might explode.

"Let's go." I said.

Once I got outside, I realized I was now limping like Don Jacinto. I had a sullen look and a budding beard. We climbed into the Chevrolet, and while I took down the cardboard, I asked them why they'd attacked the maid so savagely.

"So that wasn't Don Jacinto's daughter?" asked Beti, surprised.

I said no, they'd made a mistake. The girl was at school. They exchanged glances.

I started the car and went to look for a quiet place to park and rest after so much excitement, but I couldn't find one anywhere. We went downtown, to the buildings destroyed by the earthquake, the sidewalks packed with street vendors selling piles of used clothing from the United States, the sound of hundreds of stereos playing at the same time, and the crazed crowds of people pouring out onto the streets. The yellow Chevrolet moved at a snail's pace through the sea of bodies. It was hard to believe that what had once been the historic city centre had now been plunged into chaos, only as a result of the government's indolence. I wanted to do my good deed for the day and help clean up the neighbourhood. I stopped the car where the crowds were thickest and told the ladies to go out for a stroll. I was worn out and needed to be alone for a while. I opened the car door. I reached for the bottle of rum, lit a cigarette and told myself the solution was to find a group of apartment blocks like the ones where my sister Adriana lived. Somewhere where the car wouldn't be noticed for a few days. Why hadn't I thought of it before?

The din outside was tremendous. The ladies were in a kind of orgy, biting everything in sight. I had closed the door and window to block out the screaming, but I could still feel the terror of the fleeing crowds beating in my eardrums. In just a few seconds the street had been destroyed. There were dozens of bodies lying twisted on the ground between the vendors' stalls, as though there'd been a machine gun attack or an earthquake. I thought we shouldn't call too much attention to ourselves. I opened the car door and yelled for them to come back. They came in excited and out of breath. I started the car while they gossiped liked maidens in a tearoom, which was unlike them.

We went to the other end of town, near the road that led to the harbour. I found a place far away from stores, pharmacies, or any other businesses. It was on a street near a row of newly built houses, most of them probably still empty, let alone equipped with a phone line. I turned the car off, put up the cardboard, took the beat-up address book from the glove compartment and headed out to find a phone booth. I had to walk about ten blocks. I looked under the A's and found the late Aurora's number. I dialled but no one answered. This could mean one of two things: either the guy was at work, or he didn't live there anymore. Once again, I had nothing to do. I needed a newspaper (had there been any reports that two indigents had died in a scuffle?) and my television, but I couldn't go back to my sister's and face her questioning. I decided it was a good time to read the letters and newspaper clippings. The ladies had disappeared. I turned on the flashlight and made myself comfortable, with the cigarettes and rum nearby. First I read what the papers had to say. In the briefs section, I found the story. Mrs. Aurora Pineda, a secretary at the Steel Tube Company, had been murdered while coming home from work by a pair of thieves who snatched her purse, which contained her pay cheque, as well as her wristwatch and a necklace. It seemed the victim had fought back and the criminals shot her in the head. There were no witnesses. That was all. I was surprised that it had happened just three years ago. I quickly arranged the seven letters in chronological order. She was the pretentious type, with no notion of spelling or grammar. She'd be a useless secretary, unless you were sleeping with her. She was also an opportunist – she asked Don Jacinto to buy her clothes and trinkets and to pay her debts. In the fifth letter, her tone changed. She was worried because her husband suspected something. He was watching her. She scolded Don Jacinto for not taking her seriously, for not wanting to divorce his wife and marry her. In the sixth letter, she was no longer worried, but scared. Her husband had found out. A friend of his had seen her in Don Jacinto's car during business hours. She talked about beatings and death threats. In the seventh letter her fear had turned into terror. She said Raúl had sworn that after he killed her, he'd ruin Don Jacinto. I spent some time turning it all over in my head, picturing this idiot woman getting herself involved in a passionate affair that got out of hand. I tried to figure out how Raúl had ruined Don Jacinto's life, besides murdering his mistress. I stayed there wondering, mulling over different hypotheses until I fell asleep.

When I woke up, it was already dark. The ladies had left their hiding places and were sleeping peacefully. I went back to the phone booth. This time a man answered.

"Good evening. I'm calling from the telephone company," I said. "This is a routine check. Is this 225-4435, the residence of Don Raúl Pineda?"

"That's right," he said.

"Your address, please."

It turned out that we were fairly close, about half an hour's walk away. The yellow Chevrolet was sitting in its spot, where it would spend that night, the next one, and as far into the future as possible. I'd left the bottle of rum in the car, but I needed it for the trip, so I went back to get it, without thinking of inviting them along. Limping, I covered the distance to a residential area with tiny houses built close together – the cells of the masses. The driveways all looked alike, and they were packed with loud groups of people, as though everyone wanted to spend the night out under the stars. I stopped in front of the house. There was music and loud laughter coming from inside. I rang the doorbell. Soon a man came to the door, eager, and certain that I was the guy they'd been waiting for. His expression changed when he took in my appearance. I could see at least half a dozen men making a racket and drinking around a table, under a thick cloud of smoke that reeked of marijuana.

"Is Gustavo here?" I asked before raising the bottle of rum to my lips.

"Gustavo? Gustavo who?"

"Gustavo," I repeated. "He told me to meet him for a drink at this address."

Clearly, this guy wasn't the owner of the house.

"Hey, Raúl, do you know someone called Gustavo?" he shouted. But the others paid no attention to him.

They were laughing, toasting each other, all talking at once. Finally a stocky, medium-sized guy got up and came to the door.

"He says Gustavo invited him."

"Gustavo who?"

The other man shrugged his shoulders. No one here knew anybody called Gustavo. I had the wrong address and I should leave. They closed the door in my face. I knocked again. Raúl opened the door. He stood on the threshold, menacing.

"What the hell do you want?"

I took another sip and nodded towards the inside of the house.

"Are you Don Raúl Pineda?" I asked.

He seemed confused and turned to look over at his buddies.

"Yeah, that's me," he said. "Get to the point. I'm busy here."

"I have some letters," I mumbled. "Letters sent by Mrs. Aurora Pineda to Don Jacinto Bustillo, both deceased, incidentally. I wanted to know if you were interested . . ."

His face changed. Without a word, he grabbed me by the lapels and hauled me over to the table where the others were drinking. They jumped up and took out their guns.

"Get this motherfucker!" He screamed, enraged.

They picked me up by the arms and started beating me. "No one fucking blackmails me!" he shouted in between kicks and punches. They dropped me on the floor, beaten but still conscious. Raúl grabbed my hair, dragged me over to the door and kicked me out onto the street. "Next time I kill you, you piece of shit!" He came over again and booted me in the ribs.

I stayed there, lying on the street, my face swollen and bloody, unable to breathe or move. I moaned and spit out a couple of teeth. I managed to get on my hands and knees to vomit. Everything was spinning. Finally, I got up, stumbling and balancing myself against trees, walls, and cars. I passed groups of people who moved away from me, whispering as I walked by. I needed a drink but my bottle had dropped when he'd dragged me into the house. I left the neighbourhood. I was disoriented. I staggered to one of those gas stations with a supermarket attached to it and an enormous parking lot. It was full of cars and teenagers drinking and shouting over the roar of their sound systems. I looked for a faucet to drink some water and splash my face. I lay down on some grass to rest when a smiling, drunk fat guy came over to piss next to me and decided to take advantage of my unfortunate condition.

"Let's see if you grow some branches," he said, laughing as he doused me with his steaming piss.

"You shit," I said, and tried to get up.

"What did you say!" he yelled. He came closer and aimed the stream in my face. I tried to cover myself with my hands. Furious, he shook it off, spit at me and kicked me a few times. I rolled backwards, even though my whole body ached. I hobbled over to a side street, wiping my face with my shirt, and headed down the road that would lead me back to my yellow Chevrolet. I climbed into the car, completely shattered, and looked for more rum. Without even turning on the flashlight, I let my body fall, hoping to sleep until the next day. But Beti was awake.

"What happened to you?" she asked.

I told her I'd gone to find Don Jacinto's mistress's husband, that he'd beaten me to a pulp and later, at a gas station, a fat guy had pissed on me. She was indignant. How could I have gone to find that man without taking them? I didn't know what to say. I just wanted to rest. The other three were awake now and they pressed for more details. I told them about my ordeal, but as I talked, my pain and exhaustion turned into rage. I hadn't even been able to use my pocketknife. Assholes.

"Let's go settle the score with those people," Carmela said decisively. She didn't want to stop and discuss it and the others were just as riled up.

I got on the stool, took the cardboard off the windshield and took off towards the gas station. I stopped the car at the entrance of the parking lot. I opened the car door and told them the fat guy was with that group over there. I took another swig of rum and lit a cigarette. It was a Friday night and the fun was about to begin. I'd never seen the ladies so furious. Carmela did a somersault and coiled herself around the fat guy's neck so hard she nearly took his head off. The other three bit him before turning on his friends. The terror spread instantly. Some people were rushing into their cars; others were running to hide in the supermarket. Many didn't even know what had caused the stampede. I took out my pocketknife and cleaned the dirt out from under my fingernails. In all the confusion, several cars collided trying to escape. A long-haired guy who'd been bitten managed to climb into his brand-new car and tear out at full speed, but lost control and smashed into the gas pumps. First there was a series of small explosions. Then there was a roar so loud I was afraid the explosion would fry the Chevrolet. The ladies scrambled inside, terrified by the fire. I put the car in reverse and managed to get out of the chaos. We headed to Raúl Pineda's house. Slowly, the ladies regained their composure. I parked in the entrance of the driveway.

"Be careful. These guys have guns," I warned before turning off the car. Loli turned and looked at me doubtfully. "All four of you don't have to go," I said. I wanted a drink, but I'd already finished all the rum that was left. We got out. None of the ladies stayed behind. The groups of people had already broken up. There were only a few couples here and there in the driveways, talking. I told them to make sure no one saw them; otherwise, there'd be such a fuss the men inside would escape.

I rang the bell and moved to the side of the door. One of the men opened it without asking who was there.

Beti bit his hand. In a fraction of a second, the four of them threw themselves at him and all the people inside, who'd barely got to their feet. They were terrified, perhaps thinking that this was all a hallucination caused by too much mixing of booze and marijuana. I peeked inside, but I didn't see Raúl among the convulsing bodies. He must have been in the bathroom. He'd probably barricaded himself there, thinking that a bunch of his enemies had attacked the house. I stealthily went inside and closed the door behind me. I grabbed all the bottles that were on the table, and was lucky enough to find several bags of marijuana and cocaine there, too. The silence was intense. The men couldn't complain; their tongues were too stiff. All they could do was foam at the mouth. The ladies looked at me questioningly.

"Raúl is missing," I mouthed, pointing at what I thought was the bathroom door. The ladies went into formation, ready to attack. I told them to keep quiet and not move their tails, especially Valentina. I hid under the table, because I knew Raúl wouldn't come out without a gun. I took a big sip of rum and waited. Over a minute passed. The lock on the door started to turn very slowly, very carefully. But Valentina couldn't contain herself. Alerted by her hissing, he came out shooting, running towards the back bedroom. The blasts frightened the ladies. A shot blew Valentina's head apart.

"Help!" Raúl managed to yell just seconds before Carmela flew onto his neck. He fired again, but Beti caught his wrist. I took his gun, stuck it under my shirt and ran to the door. Loli stopped, seemingly paralyzed in front of Valentina's corpse. She started to cry uncontrollably.

"Let's go!" I yelled.

When I got to the driveway, carrying Valentina's destroyed remains, several neighbours were peeking out through their windows and half-opened doors, but they disappeared as soon as they saw the other three ladies slithering behind me. We got to the yellow Chevrolet and left, heads bowed in sadness. The execution of Raúl Pineda was worth nothing compared to the death of our most beloved and beautiful Valentina.

I went back to the spot I'd left less than an hour before. I was overcome with despair – the beating, the wealth of emotions and the death of Valentina had devastated me. I barely managed to put the cardboard back up in the windshield and find a place for my blanket before I fell asleep next to Valentina's body. I had a strange dream that I tried to interpret with the help of the ladies the next morning. Don Jacinto (who was really me), Doña Sofía, their daughter, and Raúl Pineda were in a room lying on a bed. Pineda made love to the mother and then to the girl, but I didn't react or feel the slightest bit of pain or disgust. It was as though I were watching an enjoyable movie, until Valentina appeared and wrapped her provocative body around me in an indescribably slippery, orgasmic embrace.

I woke up in pain. My body was one big bruise. The ladies were in their hiding places, obviously exhausted by the previous evening's activities. I wondered what we'd do with Valentina's corpse. I got out of the car and stretched. It was early. I looked for a newsboy to buy the paper. To my huge surprise, I saw that we were on the front page. The headline read SNAKE INVASION and below that, CHAOS IN THE CITY: DOZENS DEAD AND INJURED. A picture of the gas station in flames covered most of the front page and beside it were two small photographs of the posh lady from the mall and the line of bodies at Raúl Pineda's house. I hurried back to the car.

"Look at this!" I shouted once I'd got back in the yellow Chevrolet. "We're on the front page!" The ladies didn't understand my joy. "We're important!" I insisted. "We're in all the headlines. Don't you know what this means?"

They were on tenterhooks. I knew it would make no sense to try to convince them of the importance of being front-page news – a privilege normally reserved for politicians, criminals, and similar people. The ladies showed no interest in being a part of that riffraff. But there we were, nearly dominating the national news section. There were articles and interviews with witnesses who described deadly snakes, a bearded beggar and a yellow Chevrolet. I read a statement by Deputy Commissioner Lito Handal, who was in charge of the investigation,

43

with particular interest. "Due to the unusual nature of the crimes, Handal believes they may be the work of a criminal mastermind, probably an insane snake charmer," the article read. "The Deputy Commissioner assured the public that there are already solid clues leading to the perpetrators of these heinous acts," it continued. "He stated that the night before last, an officer attempted to detain the occupant of a Chevrolet similar to the one described by witnesses, but that the suspect managed to flee the scene." There were two small photographs of Officer Dolores Cuéllar and Niña Beatriz Díaz, who said the car in question had been parked in front of Mrs. Díaz's store for two weeks, but that after Officer Cuéllar's inspection two nights ago, the yellow Chevrolet had disappeared. Further on, the reporter mentioned me by name as a probable victim who had been kidnapped by the owner of the car and of the snakes. I felt flattered. It was the first time in my life that I'd ever been in the newspaper. On another page there was a sketch of the man with the snakes and the yellow Chevrolet. It was a combination of Don Jacinto's face and my own. The most shocking picture inside had been taken in the downtown area.

I was delighted. I forgot all about the ladies, my aching bones and Valentina's body. How could we have caused such a commotion in so little time? I read all the information on our whereabouts. The editorial called for a tightening of the city's security to prevent just any madman from plunging it into chaos. There was another article on the murder of Doña Sofía Bustillo, who had been savagely stabbed in her home. Her maid was also dead, but she was a victim of multiple snakebites. Based on that information, Deputy Commissioner Handal believed the crime was connected to the events that had shaken the public. The most sinister part of the investigation was the "massacre" of seven detectives from the Intelligence and Narcotics Department (DICA) including Chief Detective Raúl Pineda, in whose home the officers had been attacked by snakes.

"Ladies," I said, "I think we're going to have to hibernate for a while. Everyone must be looking for our yellow Chevrolet right now."

I took the cardboard down from the windshield and the windows. Two people were already looking at the car from the sidewalk. When they saw me moving around, they went down the road. I needed to find a covered garage or a reliable repair shop to leave the Chevrolet for a few days, until people forgot about all this and we could drive around the streets again. We took advantage of the early hour and headed out of the city, looking for the road that led to the top of the volcano. I was in luck – I didn't run into any police cars. Few cars drove around this rural area dotted with enormous mansions that belonged to politicians and the filthy rich. As I passed an enormous stone wall, behind which the top of a large mansion could be seen, I saw that the iron gate was being opened automatically. I manoeuvred so quickly the guard had no time to react. I rammed him and he fell across the windshield. I stopped the Chevrolet by crashing it into a Mercedes Benz that was getting ready to leave the property. A bodyguard jumped out of the back seat holding a submachine gun. I threw myself to the car floor, opened the door and shouted to the ladies to be careful. The bodyguard shot out the windshield, but was quickly neutralized by Carmela. The driver tried to back up, but Beti was already inside the car. An elegant-looking man, like the kind you see on television, got out of the car and ran towards the mansion, but Loli got him before he reached the door. The guard was lying on the ground, badly wounded and terrified at the sight of Beti. I asked him how to close the gate. There was a remote control in the Mercedes, he stammered, on the ceiling behind the sunroof. The driver was convulsing.

"What a garden!" I yelled.

There were two more gleaming cars in front of the mansion. Hysterical screams were coming from the front rooms. I hurried in. Beti bit the guard and slipped ahead of me. "That's Don Abraham Ferracuti . . ." I said, stepping over the body of the famous politician and banker, who was much more purple and contorted than he looked on the TV news. Two maids were rolling around on the floor of an incredibly luxurious room, the likes of which I'd only ever seen in movies. A beautiful older

46

lady, wrapped in a silk dressing gown, was howling in pain on the stairs, a cordless telephone at her feet. The young girl who had locked herself in her room was screaming at the top of her lungs. She must have been trying to call for help, I thought. I took out Raúl Pineda's gun and shot out the lock. Beti angrily turned to face me, as though my firing bothered her. I pushed the door open and just as I thought, the young girl was dialling the phone with trembling hands. She stopped when she saw Beti.

"Get that animal out of here! Help!" she screamed, and threw the phone at Beti. She was naked, just out of the bath, her blonde hair still dripping. She was lovelier than any woman I'd ever been with. But Beti didn't let me fantasize. She bit her over and over again on the calves, the thighs and the neck. I was amazed at how quickly her body became disfigured. I went downstairs. There was a place set in the dining room. A coffeemaker bubbled in the kitchen. Carmela was in front of the door to the servants' area.

"Two women locked themselves up in there," she grumbled.

I fired the gun again. It wasn't hard to find the old nanny and a young girl, this one even more beautiful than the other.

"Please don't hurt us!" she begged, less arrogant than her sister. The old lady got down on her knees, crossed herself and began to pray. Carmela seemed unfamiliar with these rituals. She did a pirouette and wrapped herself around the old lady's neck. The girl fainted and Carmela bit her on the thigh.

There was no one left. I went back to the Chevrolet. But in that instant, two dogs who must have hidden when they heard the first shot appeared. Loli climbed into the car as if she were being chased by the devil himself. Beti and Carmela turned to face them. The dogs growled menacingly and the ladies hissed, their heads raised and their tongues out. I was afraid this would end badly. I told them it would be best if they got in the car. My attempt to use this house as a hiding place had failed; with so many shots fired, more than one neighbour would have called the police. I shot one of the dogs. The other one ran off. I reached into the Mercedes to open the iron gate with the remote control. We took off for the city to make sure Deputy Commissioner Handal didn't catch us in the upper part of the volcano.

"Relax, it's over now," I said to Loli. I could see she was still frightened.

"I hate those animals," she said.

I lit a cigarette.

"They're not that bad," said Beti.

"We could've finished them off," mumbled Carmela, and looked at me reproachfully, as though I'd forced them to get back in the car.

"I'm not so sure," I said. "I could tell you were hesitating."

The Chevrolet attracted even more attention now that it had no windshield. I stopped at a phone booth. I called the police and asked for Deputy Commissioner Handal. It wasn't long before he was on the line.

"Deputy Commissioner Handal?"

"Who's speaking?" His voice was hoarse and intimidating.

"The snakes just attacked Doctor Abraham Ferracuti's house," I said nervously. "On the street that goes up the volcano."

"What!"

"I'm a neighbour," I continued. "I saw the old yellow car they described in the newspaper go to the doctor's house. Then there were shots. Then the car left and headed up the street."

"Give me your name and address."

"Arquímides Batres," I said. "225 Volcán Street."

"We're on our way."

I got back in the Chevrolet. I drove aimlessly, my mind a complete blank. Some drivers looked at me with curiosity, others with hostility, and still others with obvious terror, as if they recognized us. I took a long drink of rum to try to clear my mind. I kept to little side streets to see if anyone was following us. Then I had a brilliant idea. We should go to a scrapyard, the only place where we could safely spend the night without anyone noticing the yellow Chevrolet. We looked for one, and by coincidence, we found it in the same area as the Bustillo family home. It was enormous, with a single entrance and a little booth with a security guard who let me pass without asking a thing.

"The office is over there," he said, pointing.

We went in the direction he indicated, but didn't stop. I continued all the way to the far side of the lot, where I parked the yellow Chevrolet in the middle of a pile of old wrecks that camouflaged it perfectly. I waited a while to see if any employees came around, but the atmosphere was relaxed and gave the impression that they only paid attention to the cars that were leaving.

"It's time to do something about Valentina," I said.

This saddened them. In the excitement of the last few hours, they'd forgotten about their friend. I took out my pocketknife and slit her from the mouth to the tip of her tail. I skinned her as delicately as I could. She was still smooth. Then I cut her up. I gave the ladies some pieces of her meat to wolf down and put the rest of her flesh in the cans Don Jacinto had collected so that I could roast it later on.

TWO

"Quit pulling my leg, I'm not in the mood," Deputy Commissioner Lito Handal grumbled, as he leaned back in his swivel chair, his feet up on the desk, cleaning his ear with his little finger. It was Friday afternoon. He was starving and ready to go home. But the officer on the other end of the line insisted he wasn't joking; that was the report he'd received: four deaths from snakebites at the Plaza Morena mall. "Some clown is having a laugh." He hung up.

But as soon as he'd put the phone down, it rang again. It was the Commissioner. He sat up. He couldn't believe it: his boss was telling him to go down to the mall immediately and investigate. "The report is pretty bizarre, sir," he said. "This snake business is hard to believe." But the Commissioner didn't want his opinion; he was ordering him to take charge of the investigation. One of the victims was Doña Estela Ferracuti Linz, Dr. Abraham Ferracuti's younger sister. Wasn't that serious enough for him? Handal called in his two assistants, detectives Flores and Villalta. "Have you heard this crap?" he asked them, as he put on his jacket. He was a dumpy guy of medium height who was always perfectly clean-shaven but hated wearing a tie.

"There must be a lot of witnesses, boss," said Flores, a thin guy with pale skin and light-coloured eyes.

Villalta handed the Deputy Commissioner a folder, rubbed his large jaw and wheezed in his high-pitched voice, "We've got a description of the suspect and his car."

What about the snakes, Handal thought.

They hurried down the staircase of the police headquarters, known as the Black Palace, went to the parking lot and got into the Deputy Commissioner's Nissan. Villalta drove; Flores sat in the back seat. It was too hot, the rush hour traffic was at its worst and the air conditioning in the Deputy Commissioner's car wasn't working. Villalta put the siren on.

The report Handal read was straightforward: a man in his fifties who looked like a beggar had come to the mall in a beat-up old American car. When security guards asked him to leave, he let his snakes out to attack them. Then he went down the supermarket aisles, sending shoppers and employees into a panic. "It doesn't say how many snakes there were," he said, spitting out the window onto the pavement. He had heartburn and he was hoping that all of this was nothing more than a misunderstanding so he could go home and have a good meal.

When they got to the mall, the bodies were still lying there. The judge had been delayed, explained an officer; they expected him any minute now so he could start examining the crime scene.

"I want to talk to all the witnesses," ordered Handal, digging into his ear with his little finger.

"There are dozens of them, sir," said the sergeant who'd been in charge.

"It doesn't matter. I want all of them in my office this afternoon. And make sure those security guards come, too. Right away."

Handal examined the body in the parking lot. Then he went into the mall, where Mrs. Ferracuti was lying, covered with a sheet. Some of the members of her family had already arrived.

"Are you in charge here?" a distinguished-looking older man asked. It was Dr. Abraham Ferracuti.

"Yes, sir," said Handal.

"Do you know who I am?"

"Yes, sir."

"You can't leave my sister lying here," he said indignantly.

"We have to wait for the judge to come and examine the scene," the Deputy Commissioner explained, as he lifted the sheet. Despite the effects of the venom, she still looked elegant and beautiful. "I'm sorry, I'm not authorized to let them take the body away." Handal respectfully excused himself and made his way to the supermarket.

"I want you to look up every pet store and veterinarian and find out who keeps snakes as pets," he told detective Flores.

The security guard's body was lying near the entrance of the supermarket and the youth who'd been strangled was next to the meat counter.

"Get Forensics to talk to everyone here so they can make a composite sketch of the suspect and get me more details about his car right away," he told Villalta.

The swollen and disfigured bodies had taken away his appetite for the moment, but not his heartburn. He had a feeling this would be a complicated case that would force him to work more than he could bear.

Half an hour later they returned to police headquarters, followed by a couple of patrol cars carrying witnesses. Villalta drove the Nissan. He hadn't been able to get any more details about the suspect's car, except that it was old and yellow and its windows were covered with pieces of cardboard. Flores had gone with another group of officers to look up pet stores and vets.

The Deputy Commissioner went inside and asked someone to order him a hamburger, fries and a coke. He told himself he'd get a proper dinner that night. He started questioning the witnesses right away: the security guard who'd managed to escape from the parking lot, another who'd hidden in the supermarket and a third who'd taken a shot at the suspect. He also questioned the saleswoman from the boutique Mrs. Ferracuti had been coming out of, as well as a couple of bystanders – customers from the supermarket who wanted to help out. Nothing was clear, not even the number of reptiles involved. Some said there were six, others said ten. No one could give any specific details. The only new information he got was from the first security guard, who said the suspect reeked of alcohol.

Detective Flores came in looking discouraged.

"No one in the city breeds snakes, boss."

The Deputy Commissioner leaned back in his swivel chair and put his feet up on the desk.

"A beat-up old car, a drunken bum and a half dozen snakes just to take out the sister of one of the most powerful men in the country . . . it just doesn't make sense. It doesn't sound right," he mumbled.

The phone rang. It was Villalta. They'd finished the composite sketch of the suspect, but he had some news. Two murders had just been reported in San Mateo, a nearby suburb, and one of the victims had been practically chewed up by snakes.

The Deputy Commissioner jumped out of his chair.

"Let's go!" he shouted, and took out his radio handset.

The Commissioner had already called a second time to check on the progress of the case, which meant the pressure from above would only get worse.

"Does the name Bustillo sound familiar to you, boss?" asked Villalta. He didn't put the siren on, but he drove at full speed anyway, running red lights and zooming past any car that tried to cross his path.

"Not at all," Handal answered. "Are there any survivors?"

"Not exactly. They killed a Mrs. Bustillo and a maid. Her daughter found the bodies when she came back from school," explained Villalta. "It doesn't look like anything was stolen."

Two patrol cars were already parked in front of the house and a group of onlookers were crowded around the front door.

Handal stopped in front of Mrs. Bustillo's body. An amateur job, he thought. He walked over to the maid. He had a feeling that the key to the entire case lay here, or at least the only clue to solving it. Apart from the bodies, the house was in perfect order, as if nothing had been touched.

"Where's the girl?" he asked. "I want to talk to her."

An officer told him she was at a neighbour's. She was in total shock; he'd have to wait a few hours before he could question her, at least until the sedatives had taken effect.

"I'll try if you want, boss," said Flores, who was known as the station's smooth-talker – extremely useful for getting information from both witnesses and suspects. He was one of the brand-new detectives trained after the war; he looked like a nice guy and had good gringo manners.

The Deputy Commissioner stuck his little finger in his ear.

"All right," he said. "And you, go and see what you can get out of the neighbours, especially whether they saw an old, yellow American car hanging around," he told Villalta. He went over to the Nissan, picked up the radio and asked to speak to the chief of forensics. He told him he wanted the results of the tests to see if the snakes involved in the incident at the shopping mall were the same as those who'd attacked this unfortunate maid, and he wanted them now. Then he walked to the neighbour's house to see what Flores had found out.

The girl wasn't hysterical anymore. Her name was Sofía, just like her late mother. She'd just turned sixteen. That afternoon, she'd come home from school just as she did every other day, and had walked into a gruesome crime scene.

"Did you notice anything unusual near the house?" asked Flores. "Were there any cars parked out front?"

No, she couldn't think of anyone who would want to hurt her mother; they didn't have any enemies, she said, sniffling. Yes, of course, they lived alone with the maid. Her father? He left them about three years ago. Her mother acted as if he were dead, as if he'd never existed, but the girl still hoped she'd see him again. No, she didn't know where he was. He used to be an accountant at a company. How were they supporting themselves? They owned a chain of pharmacies called La Surtidora that they'd inherited from her grandfather.

"Where is it?" asked the Deputy Commissioner.

The biggest location was downtown, she explained, and there was another pharmacy at the Plaza Morena mall. Flores turned to look at his boss.

"Do you know anyone who has anything to do with snakes?" he asked.

No, she couldn't think of anyone, she said. Villalta hurried into the room. He looked at the girl – at sixteen she was already a good-looking young woman – and then at the Deputy Commissioner.

"A neighbour says he saw a yellow car parked in front of the house," he said in his high-pitched voice. "He can't remember the make, but it was a beat-up old American model." Handal snapped his fingers. "We've got him," he said. "Let's get back to headquarters."

But the girl had her mouth open in shock.

"No, it can't be," she whispered.

"What can't be?" Handal asked, grabbing her arm.

"No, it's impossible!" she screamed and started to cry uncontrollably. Her father had a yellow Chevrolet, she managed to stammer. It was an old model, just like the one he'd had when he was young. It was the only thing he took with him when he left.

They raced out.

"I want everything we have on file about this Jacinto Bustillo," Handal ordered Flores, before turning to Villalta. "Call headquarters and get them to look in the records for all the information we've got on the yellow Chevrolet."

Villalta ran to the Nissan and grabbed the radio. Flores stayed at the Bustillo home to look for clues. They were about to get to the bottom of things, thought Handal, and luckily, it looked like Mrs. Ferracuti's death was accidental. He got in the car. He asked to be patched through to the Commissioner. It was urgent. He told him the evidence was pointing to a nut called Jacinto Bustillo. It was a crime of passion and unfortunately, Dr. Ferracuti's sister was in the wrong place at the wrong time. That was all.

He'd just hung up when he was called on the radio again. There was an emergency on the corner of Fifth Avenue and Darío Street, in the heart of the crowded downtown area. A massive snake attack had caused multiple injuries and deaths. Villalta put on the siren.

"We've got to catch this son-of-a-bitch before he drives the whole city insane," Handal mumbled. He put two and two together and called the Black Palace to find out where the Bustillo family pharmacy was located. He was right: it was on Darío Street, right near Fifth Avenue, the operator said. Stabbing his wife didn't seem to have satisfied Bustillo.

Getting to the crime scene was going to be a feat in itself. Traffic was a nightmare. Sirens were blaring in all directions. Police cars, ambulances, and fire fighters were trying unsuccessfully to get to the victims. People were running, terrified.

"Snake attack!"

Drivers were getting out of their cars to ask what was going on. Then they'd rush back inside, roll up the windows and try to escape by driving on the sidewalks.

"Leave the car here," Handal ordered. "Let's walk. We'll never get there like this." Villalta looked at him distrustfully. What if the snakes were still there? They walked slowly, moving against the flow of people under the blazing sun, sweating like pigs, pistols drawn, expecting to run into snakes at every turn. But when they got to Fifth Avenue, it was clear that the snakes had gone. The only thing left behind was a devastating scene of death and chaos. Dozens of bodies lay twisted on the ground, some still convulsing, and others with swollen tongues sticking out.

The Deputy Commissioner went over to one of the two patrol cars that had managed to get to the scene. He took out the radio and ordered a red alert search for an early model yellow Chevrolet, and asked for a helicopter to search the area. Ambulances, firefighters and more police arrived on the scene. There weren't enough stretchers for all the injured people. Handal walked over to the La Surtidora pharmacy. When the violence broke out, most of the storeowners had closed the iron shutters that covered the windows. Only a few of the street vendors' stands were still upright. Pretty soon the trail of merchandise left in the street would attract bands of petty thieves. The area was cordoned off. Handal banged on the pharmacy's iron shutters.

"Police!" he called. "You can open the door. You're out of danger."

A small door opened and several frightened employees in white coats came out. They opened the iron shutters.

"Did any of you see a yellow car parked out in front here?" Handal asked.

No one had seen anything, just the stampede of people screaming in terror. They'd closed the pharmacy right away. They knew something had happened to Doña Sofía, the owner, but they didn't know any details. The manager would be back soon to tell them.

The Deputy Commissioner asked which employee had worked there longest. A woman with greying hair and a double chin said she'd been there ten years. Handal asked to speak to her in private. They went to the office at the back of the store.

"Mrs. Bustillo is dead," he blurted. "She was stabbed a couple of hours ago."

She didn't cry or faint, but seemed overwhelmed with sadness and grief. She said she'd been afraid something terrible had happened because of how abruptly the manager had left and the expression he had on his face. She'd had a feeling. Don Jacinto? Well, he'd disappeared a long time ago, more than three years now. He had an affair, the dirty scoundrel, with his own secretary, a young newlywed. Doña Sofía found out about it and asked for a divorce. The girl's husband found out too and she heard he tried to blackmail Don Jacinto. A little later, Don Jacinto's mistress was killed in a robbery and he disappeared. It was like a soap opera.

"But you don't think Don Jacinto killed Mrs. Bustillo, do you?"

"He's the prime suspect."

That was hard for her to believe. He'd seemed like such a nice, decent person, though he rarely came to the pharmacy.

Had she ever seen him again?

Never. She had no idea where he was; he was a taboo subject at the pharmacy. Once she heard that he'd become a drunken bum and was living in the slums. She hadn't seen the yellow Chevrolet and she didn't know of Bustillo having any connection with snakes, either.

The Deputy Commissioner went outside.

"Thirty-two dead, boss," Villalta said. "So far."

Plus the four from the Plaza Morena mall and the two women, all in less than four hours, thought Handal. A real massacre.

"We've got to get this nut no matter what," he grumbled. "Where the hell did he get those snakes?"

It no longer mattered now that Mrs. Ferracuti's death was accidental. With so many bodies, he didn't even want to imagine how much pressure he'd be under. He got the picture right away. An officer came to tell him that the Commissioner was on the radio. It was urgent.

Then he saw her coming. Just what he needed: god-damn Rita, with her notebook open and a photographer right behind her, ready to make his life miserable with a million questions and twist the whole story for the morning paper. As if he didn't have enough to deal with, what with this nut Bustillo roaming through the city streets with his snakes.

"Keep your mouth shut. She's not getting anything out of you," he warned Villalta before he stepped up to the microphone.

He knew what he was saying: it wouldn't have been the first time Villalta spilled his guts to a halfway decent-looking reporter. All the news outlets knew it, and since they'd found out about the detective's weakness, they'd only sent attractive girls to cover the police beat. Rita, who worked for a sensationalist paper called *Ocho Columnas* was the worst of them, with her provocative miniskirts, her slender but shapely legs, and the silk blouses she wore without a bra so you could see her nipples.

The Commissioner ordered him to get back to the Black Palace immediately and give him a report in person. The radio stations were saying that a "snake attack" had killed dozens right downtown and panic was beginning to spread through the city. What the hell was this all about? Handal anxiously stuck his little finger in his ear.

"Deputy Commissioner, is it true that the man with the snakes is driving an old yellow car?" Rita asked hurriedly.

Handal told Villalta to get the Nissan they'd left a few blocks away.

"Do you know the suspect's name? Where did he get the snakes?" the reporter insisted, running behind them.

"I can't tell you anything right now," Handal said, turning to face her. "In a couple of hours we'll hold a press conference at headquarters."

But she was stubborn.

"Is there a connection between the murder of Mrs. Bustillo and the attacks downtown at the Plaza Morena mall?"

The Deputy Commissioner quickened his pace. They got in the car and tore off at full speed. Rita stayed on the sidewalk, shouting and trying to slip her foot back into a shoe that had fallen off on the way.

They didn't talk on the ride back. Handal was mentally preparing the report he would give to the Commissioner. He climbed the stairs at headquarters in long strides. The secretary told him to go in right away. The boss was waiting for him.

"We've got him cornered," the Deputy Commissioner said, after laying out the facts and dismissing the theory that the attacks were specifically aimed at Mrs. Ferracuti. Instead, he focused on his idea that a mentally unbalanced man named Jacinto Bustillo was taking revenge on the woman he'd lived with until three years ago. "As soon as we find the car, we'll get him."

The Commissioner was beside himself. The President's private secretary had phoned him to ask what the hell was going on. They couldn't rest until they found that car. What if the guy was hiding it in a garage? They needed more clues. A drunk couldn't just wander around with half a dozen snakes in a Chevrolet. Any minute now, he'd show up at another mall and kill a dozen more people. Did that not seem like a lot to him? The press was putting pressure on them; they needed to make a statement, to say something to calm everyone down.

The Deputy Commissioner swallowed a mouthful of saliva. He felt like the hole in the pit of his stomach was growing and he knew that in a few minutes he'd be under attack by a horde of reporters who were only interested in getting him to contradict himself; to say exactly the things he wasn't supposed to say. He went down to his office. Villalta and Flores were waiting for him.

"What did you get on Bustillo?" he asked the smooth-talker.

Flores repeated the same story Handal had got from the lady at the pharmacy. Also, Bustillo had two brothers, an architect and a doctor, but they hadn't heard from him either. There wasn't a trace of the suspect.

Villalta said there was no record of a yellow Chevrolet registered under the name Jacinto Bustillo. Maybe the car was too old.

"Are you sure?" Handal asked, but he knew the mess the files were in since the latest restructuring. "I'm going to have to make a statement to the media. Commissioner's orders. Things are heating up. Nobody knows what's going on. We've got to calm everyone down."

"Boss, if we describe the car, won't we be alerting the suspect?" Flores asked.

But the description of the car had already been leaked; it would be better to make photocopies of the composite sketch, but not mention Jacinto Bustillo's name, since there still wasn't any proof.

What was strange, said Villalta, stroking his large jaw, was that the suspect hadn't gone into his ex-wife's pharmacies in either the Plaza Morena mall or downtown.

"Afraid he'd be recognized," said Handal.

"But he could have at least sent the snakes," the detective insisted.

"Maybe they're not that well trained," suggested Flores.

It was four in the afternoon when Deputy Commissioner Handal entered the Black Palace's pressroom. He was tense, right now he hated the Commissioner, a guy who was too young and too naïve for the job. A guy who was forcing him to meet with the press when he still didn't have good news to report. It was really the Public Relations Officer's job to show up here. For fifteen minutes he answered the reporters' questions as vaguely as he could and stressed whenever he had the slightest opportunity that the authorities were on the suspect's trail and that the public should stay calm and report any suspicious behaviour.

Rita was the worst of them. She was insolent, insisting on asking what the motive was for the murder of Doña Sofía Bustillo and whether that crime wasn't the key to explaining the attacks at the Plaza Morena mall and downtown, as though she already knew the Deputy Commissioner's theory about the case.

"I can't say any more, we're still investigating," Handal said curtly before leaving the room. He headed towards his office.

"A woman called claiming she has some information about the yellow Chevrolet," Flores whispered to him. They still weren't far enough away from the reporters. Her name was Beatriz Díaz. She was a storeowner in the Macrópolis housing project. She said that the car had been parked in front of her store until this morning.

Handal took a breath. He walked with Flores and Villalta to his office, sat in the swivel chair, put his feet up on the desk and waited a few minutes for the reporters to leave. He didn't want any more leaks, he warned them. He told them to go down to the car without attracting any attention; he'd meet them there in a minute.

He took the time to call his wife to tell her that he was in charge of this damned case and he wasn't sure what time he'd be home for dinner.

As soon as he got in the Nissan he ordered Villalta not to put the siren on. But he soon saw how useless his caution had been: there were news vans in front of the store already.

"Goddamn sons-of-bitches!" Handal yelled.

The woman was positively gleeful in front of all the cameras and microphones. She was leaning on the counter, surrounded by bags of candy, canned goods, rolls of toilet paper and cans of soft drinks. She said the yellow Chevrolet had been parked across the street for two weeks, and that a filthy drunk slept in it at night. During the day, he'd leave to commit God only knew what evil deeds. This morning the car had disappeared, driven no doubt by that criminal, maybe because he was afraid the police would get him. A police officer had come by just the night before last.

"A police officer came here the other night?" Rita asked. She was crowded into the tiny space, which was filling up with more and more journalists.

"Yes," said Niña Beatriz. "I called the authorities to take him away. I didn't like the look of him. But the officer was weak; the guy convinced him that sleeping in your car isn't illegal. Give me a break!"

The Deputy Commissioner stepped onto the sidewalk. Exasperated, he grabbed Villalta by the arm.

68

"Get me the names of the officers who came here last night. I want them right now."

That was exactly what the reporter from *Ocho Columnas* wanted to know, but Niña Beatriz said she could only remember that his first name was Dolores. She'd forgotten his last name.

"How did you find out about this woman?" Handal asked a reporter who'd just arrived. He was beginning to lose his temper.

"I don't know," the reporter said, shrugging his shoulders. "They just sent me."

The Deputy Commissioner ordered Flores to do whatever he could to get that old bitch in the patrol car right away. He waited on the sidewalk. Now it turned out that the police had been told about the guy with the snakes two nights ago. Just what he needed.

Detective Flores was on his way, smiling like a good boy, leading Niña Beatriz to the car, paying no attention to the onslaught of cameras, microphones and reporters. They hadn't gone four blocks before Niña Beatriz told them she'd been the one who called the media. After the other night, she didn't trust the police anymore and didn't think they'd show up.

"Are you taking me to headquarters?"

"We have to interview you, madam," said Handal. "This is a serious case. I'm in charge."

She told them they were all incompetent – they could've caught the guy last night. Why hadn't they done it? She'd even called city hall to get the municipal authorities to get rid of that bum, but they ignored her too.

"Do you have any idea what the suspect's name is?" asked the Deputy Commissioner.

She wasn't so good with names, but Don Eduardo could help them. He'd even talked to him; she'd seen them. Why didn't they ask him? He lived with his sister Adriana and her husband Damián, on the second floor of Building B.

Villalta manoeuvred quickly. The Nissan did a U-turn, tires screeching, and drove back the way they'd come. The reporters' cars driving behind them couldn't keep up.

"Hey, young man, be careful! What's the matter with him?" Niña Beatriz complained. She said she didn't understand the part about the snakes. She didn't think the animals could've been in the car the whole time without her or any of the other neighbours noticing. The Chevrolet hadn't moved in two weeks. The bum left on foot every day with a canvas bag to pick up junk.

They stopped in front of the store again.

"Take a ride around the block," Handal ordered as he got out. He went to Building B, climbed the stairs to the second floor and knocked on the first of two doors. A woman asked who it was without opening up. "Police. I'm Deputy Commissioner Handal. I'm looking for Don Eduardo."

The woman opened the door, looking distrustful. Handal showed her his ID.

70

"Eduardo isn't here," she said. "He disappeared two days ago. Come in if you like."

It was Adriana. She was worried. She'd heard about the old yellow Chevrolet on the news, the one that looked like the car that had been parked out there on the street. Eduardo had tried to talk to the owner.

"When was the last time you saw him?" Handal asked without entering.

"He left on Thursday morning and he hasn't been back since. It's really strange. Eduardo always comes back here to sleep."

The Deputy Commissioner knew that this was going to be a new development in the case, one of those new developments that complicated everything. Especially now that she was saying that her brother was unemployed with a history of behavioural problems.

"Did he happen to mention the name of the man with the car?" Handal asked. He had no expectations; he just didn't want to hear any stories about a paranoid schizophrenic or anything like that.

"Don Jacinto," she said.

The Deputy Commissioner's face lit up.

"Don't tell anyone else what you just told me," he warned. "It's very important. I'll be in touch with you. If your brother shows up, let me know right away." He gave her his card, took down her telephone number and hurried down the stairs. Villalta was waiting for him with the engine running.

"We've got him," the detective said as he was pulling out. "It's Officer Dolores Cuéllar." Niña Beatriz, who was sitting in the back next to Flores, confirmed the name. Of course, that was the good-for-nothing from the other night. She could identify him and accuse him of negligence if they put him in front of her. But Handal had something else on his mind: keeping Jacinto Bustillo's identity secret so the press couldn't tip him off. They went into the Black Palace's parking lot.

"You two get a thorough statement from this lady and from Officer Cuéllar," Handal ordered. "I'll see you in my office in half an hour."

Flores and Villalta turned to look at each other in disgust – they'd better forget their Friday night plans.

It was five after five in the evening when Handal locked himself in his office. He hung up his jacket and started pacing in front of his desk. He needed to think, to get the facts straight, to find new leads to investigate. He took out a black marker and wrote "Sequence of events" on his whiteboard. Underneath, he wrote "11:30 am to 11:45 am at Plaza Morena mall. Between 12:30 pm and 1:00 pm in San Mateo. 1:40 pm on Darío Street." Then he went over to the map of the city that was hanging on the other wall and followed the route from the store in the Macrópolis housing scheme to the other three locations. Where would he attack next? Would he attack again? If his theory was right, then the guy was obsessed with his wife and her property. That's what the facts were pointing to. He picked up the phone and asked to be patched through to Flores.

"I need a list of all of Mrs. Bustillo and her close family members' property," he said. "City homes, country estates, beach houses, whatever. Villalta can interview those two witnesses, but you take care of this."

That wasn't necessary, Flores explained. They were finishing up right now with Niña Beatriz and Officer Cuéllar. Just then, the Deputy Commissioner remembered Eduardo Sosa's disappearance, the only person who'd spoken to Jacinto Bustillo in three years. Was it just a coincidence, a completely different case, or was he Bustillo's first victim? Something else didn't fit – if the police had been to see him on Wednesday night, why did the suspect wait until Friday morning to leave the Macrópolis housing project and start his crime spree? And most troubling – where did he get those snakes from and how was he controlling them?

Handal picked up the receiver again. He wanted the chief forensic psychologist to come to his office as soon as possible and help develop a profile of Bustillo that would predict his next move and his possible hideouts. But Vargas, the head of the psych team, had already left, the secretary said. They'd better get him here right away, wherever he was, the Deputy Commissioner fumed.

Flores came in.

"There's a beach house in San Juanico," he said. "Doña Sofía's only sister lives there. That's it."

Handal ordered him to tell the authorities in San Juanico about the yellow Chevrolet and get them to watch the victim's sister's house discreetly. He asked if they'd checked on Vargas yet, but he still hadn't shown up.

"We're going to do some surveillance tonight," he said. "With this nut on the loose, I don't want any more surprises."

Flores shrugged his shoulders like someone who'd already resigned himself to the task. Handal looked at his watch. It was twenty to six. Jacinto Bustillo hadn't attacked in four hours. Where could he be? Handal decided to take advantage of the hour and go home to take a shower, have a proper dinner and relax for a while. He'd think of something while Flores and Villalta kept watch.

That was what he did; only it didn't relax him. He was worried one of his assistants would call him on his radio any minute to tell him Bustillo and his snakes had reappeared with even greater verve. But once he got in the shower and scrubbed off the dirt from the insane day, he told himself that whatever happened, happened. He'd have to study the break-up of the Bustillos' marriage in detail with that awful Vargas, if he ever showed up. Something important must have gone down to make the husband turn into some kind of bum. He ate with particular enthusiasm, like someone who'd finally got what he'd wanted most all day – a couple of smoked cutlets, some rice and mashed potatoes. Then he sat down in front of the television with his wife to watch the news and be entertained by his own stern face. He looked like a competent civil servant, even though the Commissioner had thrown him to the wolves without a second thought. Where the hell had they got this theory about a snake charmer who'd gone insane? Only someone like Villalta could feed them that garbage and get them to swallow it. And that shopkeeper Beatriz Díaz looked like she was about to have an orgasm right in front of the cameras. He couldn't believe it – there was Officer Cuéllar's mug, looking nervous but happy speaking in front of the microphones. Hadn't he been told to keep his goddamn trap shut? The good news was that the events at Plaza Morena mall and the mystery of the snakes had pushed into the background the deaths of Doña Sofía and her maid, the clues that led directly to Jacinto Bustillo. Now that the news was over, the best thing was to rest up and catch a few winks right there on the couch. If nothing happened that night, if the man with the snakes just wanted to get rid of his wife and create panic around her pharmacies, then early tomorrow morning the Deputy Commissioner would call for a manhunt in the slums, the liquor stores, and the other places Bustillo hung around.

That's when someone called on the radio.

The Deputy Commissioner got up and looked at his watch. It was twenty after nine.

"The party continues, boss," said Flores. "He blew up a gas station. The Esso near the exit to the harbour."

"What!" He rubbed his eyes. It wasn't possible. "You mean it exploded?"

"Exactly, boss. Just a few minutes ago. First the snakes attacked and then there were some explosions. There's a whole bunch of dead and injured people. Should we come and get you or do we meet you there?"

There was no time to waste. They'd meet at the gas station.

He floored it. The siren wailed while he asked himself what the connection was between Doña Sofía Bustillo and that gas station.

The chaos was impressive. You could see the flames from blocks away. The gas fumes were unbearable.

He left the Nissan about a hundred metres from the scene. He walked over to where an ambulance and a patrol car were already parked, covering his nose with a handkerchief.

"Is there any danger that more underground tanks could explode?" he asked a sergeant, who didn't pay him any attention.

It was a horrifying sight. A dozen cars were scorched by the flames and there were bodies everywhere. The intense heat kept everyone back.

An officer pointed to an anxious man who was giving orders, cursing and complaining.

"That's the manager," he said.

The Deputy Commissioner took out his badge and introduced himself.

"Of course there are more tanks underground!" the manager shouted. "That's what I'm trying to tell them, everybody needs to get away from here!"

The firefighters hadn't arrived yet, nor had detectives Flores and Villalta. The wailing sirens, the thick smoke, the crackling of the flames, the bodies, the charred cars, and the people running around crazed: they'd never seen a situation like this, not even during the war.

Then Handal saw the manager run out into the street, his back to the gas station, as if he were being followed by the devil himself. He did the same, but didn't get very far. The explosion threw him to the ground. Dammit! He felt the heat of the flames at his back. He saw how they lit up the sky. He stayed on the ground, afraid there'd be another explosion. This was the hell a madman named Jacinto Bustillo had dreamed up. He raised his head. The manager was on his feet, looking fearfully at the gas station. The Deputy Commissioner was getting up and dusting off dirt and pieces of pavement when he heard someone asking him a question.

"Are you okay, boss?"

It was Flores and Villalta. They'd arrived just before the explosion and saw the moment their boss had turned away and run.

"Ask that man if there are any more gas tanks!" he ordered Villalta, pointing at the manager. A fire truck and more ambulances arrived on the scene. It was going to be hell finding the right witness in that confusion, Flores said, still open-mouthed, watching the spectacle.

"No, boss, that was the last tank left," said Villalta.

Handal was a mess: hair dishevelled, face sweaty, shirttails out, and the knees of his pants and the elbows of his jacket torn. The case had gone beyond all reasonable limits now. Furious, the Deputy Commissioner grabbed the first witness he could find. The gas station attendant, whose uniform was spotless, said he hadn't realized what was going on until he saw the stampede of cars trying to leave the parking lot and the terrified girls screaming that snakes were attacking left, right and centre.

"But how did the explosions start?" asked Handal. He had the attendant by the arm and was shaking him as if he'd been responsible for the disaster.

He just ran without thinking or trying to see anything, as fast as his legs could carry him. He was terrified of snakes. He hadn't come back after that. He was still trembling.

"Which way did the Chevrolet go?" Handal asked, shaking him again.

Villalta clenched his big jaw and gritted his teeth menacingly.

"Talk, you son-of-a-bitch, or you're going to have problems," he threatened.

Suddenly, another explosion threw them to the ground. A gust of heat, shards of glass and pieces of metal mingled with the stench of gasoline in the air. The flames had reached a car. The attendant took the opportunity to clear off to where the manager was standing. Flores approached a group of onlookers to ask if anyone had seen the yellow Chevrolet.

The gas station's manager and assistant manager told the Deputy Commissioner that when the snakes appeared, dozens of cars tried to escape and one of them crashed into a gas pump. That's how the explosions started. But as far as they understood, most of the deaths were caused by the snake attack and not by the explosion.

A short guy with chubby cheeks had seen the yellow Chevrolet.

"I threw up all the rum I'd drunk when I realized that was the car they were talking about on TV," he told Flores. "But then it was every man for himself because it was like the snakes were coming out of nowhere. I managed to lock myself in my Volkswagen."

He told Flores and Handal that the yellow Chevrolet had been at the entrance of the parking lot and then left for the boulevard, towards Jardines de la Sabana, a nearby neighbourhood. The Commissioner ordered Villalta to ask headquarters to set up a perimeter and search the area. They had to catch this crazy son-of-a-bitch no matter what. All units should be on red alert. Handal, Villalta and Flores knew they'd better get back to the Black Palace. Bustillo would surely attack again and they needed to try to predict his next move.

Then the gas station owner's eldest son arrived. His father, a filthy-rich Lebanese guy, was out of the country. The kid was dressed like he was on his way to a party and told them that neither he nor his father had any connection to someone called Sofía Bustillo.

"Shit!" Handal shouted. The theory that Jacinto Bustillo just wanted to hurt his wife was crumbling. It looked like the suspect had gone insane.

He walked over to the Nissan and radioed a request for units to be stationed at all the bars, nightclubs and gas stations in the area. It was crazy to try to do this on a Friday night, but Bustillo liked to let his snakes out in a crowd.

He was getting ready to start the car when someone told him the Commissioner was on the line. His voice was shaking with either rage or astonishment. He'd just been informed that one of his nieces, the most beautiful one, the one he loved the most, had been killed by snakes that attacked her while she was hanging around with her high-school friends at the Esso station near the exit to the harbour. What the hell happened? He wanted an explanation right away, and it better be convincing, because his niece's body, his sister's eldest daughter, was lying there in the parking lot! What the hell had he been doing since he'd been put in charge of stopping that lunatic with the snakes?

"Sir, it's been awful," Handal stammered. "We've been working non-stop, but this guy's crazy, he's a psychopath – totally unpredictable. We know where he went. We expect to find him in the next few minutes."

The Deputy Commissioner got out of the Nissan and headed for the gas station. He walked with his head down, his hands in his pockets. He felt useless. Not just because of his appearance, but because this piece of shit was slipping away from him much too easily.

And there was the Commissioner's niece. She was easy to spot: two officers were already guarding her corpse. The girl was lying on her back. Her little miniskirt showed off her perfect but now lifeless body. A fat guy with a look of terror frozen on his face lay next to her.

Handal went to look for the man in charge of the Red Cross unit, a small guy with a bulbous nose who moved like a robot.

"How many bodies?"

He said there were thirty-one killed by snakebites, and another thirteen burned by the explosion, although that wouldn't be the final number. They still had to search through the flames. Crestfallen, Handal was getting back into the Nissan when Flores radioed him to say Bustillo and his snakes had attacked again.

"Where?" Handal asked, his adrenaline pumping. He looked at his watch – it was ten-oh-seven. In a residential area called La Primavera, about five minutes from the gas station, said Flores, in a DICA agent's home. They were almost there.

"Godammit!" the Deputy Commissioner shouted.

The case was getting more complicated. Now another department was involved. There was a possibility he'd be replaced as head of the investigation. He needed to come up with a plan to surround the area immediately. The suspect probably hadn't slipped away yet. He made a mental calculation – if he attacked the gas station at a quarter after nine, he must have reached the detective's house by nine-thirty at the latest, so by now he could have left the area.

Villalta was waiting for him in the driveway in front of the DICA agent's house.

"He's turned into a real bastard, boss," he said while they walked to the house. "There are seven dead DICA agents in there. All of them killed by snakebites."

This was going to turn into a maelstrom soon. As the head of the Criminal Investigation Unit (DIC), Handal understood the rivalry between his men and their DICA counterparts only too well – bureaucratic disputes over leadership, over the allocation of resources. The narcotics agents were the golden boys, arrogant and spoiled by the gringos. The case was heating up.

"They aren't here yet?" Handal asked, picturing

Chele Pedro, the chief of DICA, appropriating the evidence and trying to take over the investigation. Villalta said no. They went inside. The scene was grotesque. There were bodies lying all over the living and dining rooms, as though victims of a gangland execution. The Deputy Commissioner checked the bodies, saw what was left of the cocaine and marijuana on the table, and went to the bedroom to have a look at the body of Raúl Pineda, the leader of the group.

"There were shots fired, according to the neighbours," said Flores.

"They showed this one no mercy," said Handal. Pineda's tongue was an enormous lump. It looked as if all the venom had concentrated in that one spot. The Deputy Commissioner spotted the blood in front of the bathroom door and the drops that led out to the street. "They got Bustillo," he added, after verifying that none of the bodies had any gunshot or knife wounds.

"More like one of the snakes," Flores said. "A neighbour says he saw the suspect leaving carrying a reptile with its head blown off."

"Obviously Pineda was the guy Bustillo and his pets were looking for," Villalta ventured in his high-pitched voice.

Handal got a flash, a feeling, an unmistakable intuition – something that wouldn't hold up with just the evidence they had so far, but was there, waiting to be discovered.

"Let's go!" he ordered.

They hurried out of the driveway when they ran into Chele Pedro and his squad, a dozen men in black uniforms carrying M-16 rifles.

"What happened?" the head of DICA asked.

"The snakes," said Handal, barely stopping.

"What do you mean, the snakes?"

But he was in a rush. He had no time to explain.

"I'll see you at headquarters," he said, walking on.

Before they got into their cars, he ordered Flores to get a detailed file on narcotics agent Raúl Pineda, and Villalta to ask Bustillo's relatives for the name of the woman he had an affair with.

He passed the gas station on the way back. The firefighters had managed to put out the flames, but the whole place reeked. That bastard Bustillo: he loved distracting them before he attacked his real target. Of course! They had to step up the surveillance in the bars and clubs, an attack there would be just what he needed.

The atmosphere at headquarters was anxious, the way it was during the war, when the sight of Handal climbing the staircase commanded more respect. He went into his office and then to the washroom to clean off the grime and to change. He always kept a spare change of clothes. Refreshed, he sat down in his swivel chair, put his feet up on the desk, stuck his left finger deep in his ear and looked at the clock. It was ten-forty-eight.

Then the phone rang. Just what he needed – Rita. She'd been to the gas station and was just leaving Raúl Pineda's house. What was behind the attacks? What was the link between the events at noon and those this evening? Was there a connection between Mrs. Bustillo and Agent Pineda?

"I've been asking myself the same questions, sweetheart," Handal said reluctantly. "I promise to have an answer for you early tomorrow." He hung up.

Flores came in carrying a folder with Pineda's background information. The Deputy Commissioner knew what he was looking for: "Marital status: widower," it said. Next to that it said the agent's wife had been killed in a mugging three years earlier. He threw the folder on the desk, satisfied and smiling. Here was the first confirmation of the intuition he'd had about the case. Now he just needed Villalta to bring him a first name, it didn't matter which, and a very specific last name.

"What's going on, boss?" Flores asked. "Did you find something?"

Handal got up, went to the whiteboard, erased what he'd written that afternoon, took out a marker and wrote "Jacinto Bustillo" in the middle. Then he put the names "Sofía Bustillo," "Raúl Pineda," and "? Pineda" next to it.

"The narcotics agent's wife was the mistress of the psychopath we're looking for," he explained. "I'm sure of it. Everything fits. We just need to confirm the name."

"But, why did he attack the gas station?" Flores asked.

To distract them, to throw the investigation off, or just for the lunatic murderer's pure pleasure – what mattered was the revenge. A crime of passion committed three years after the fact.

"Go see Narcotics," he told Flores. "See if anyone there remembers Pineda's wife's name and whether she worked as a secretary at the Steel Tube Company. And look in the files for muggings reported on this day," he added, opening the folder and pointing to the date. He sat back down in his swivel chair. He felt calmer because the basic motive for the crimes had been found. Now they just needed to arrest that crazy piece of shit. He knew that no matter what, he'd have a sleepless night. He looked at the messages on his desk. One said that Vargas, the chief forensic psychologist, was out of the city and would be back only on Monday. He leafed through the folders of the day's reports: the bodies of two homeless men who'd fought each other with knives and broken bottles were found with no identification that morning in an alley in the red-light district.

The clock struck eleven.

He called Adriana Sosa to ask if her brother had come back yet. She answered the phone anxiously, because she'd been waiting for some news from Eduardo, but she still hadn't heard from him. As soon as they got their hands on Bustillo they'd find out whether he had anything to do with the young man's disappearance, the Deputy Commissioner told himself.

Flores got back to him with the information he was looking for right away – there was a report in the files that stated Mrs. Aurora Pineda, secretary at the Steel Tube Company, had been shot and killed by two thieves. Villalta had gone and disturbed Bustillo's daughter in the middle of her mother's wake. She told him she remembered that the bitch her father had got mixed up with was called Aurora or something like that. But Handal wasn't ready to claim victory yet, much less call the Commissioner without having Bustillo in handcuffs and some minced snake meat.

"Let's go for a drive," he ordered.

They were on their way down the stairs when they ran into Chele Pedro and his squad. Overbearing, pot-bellied and double-chinned, the DICA chief blocked his path.

"What's going on here?" he demanded.

The Deputy Commissioner explained the facts of the Bustillo case, especially his relationship with Agent Pineda's late wife. He told him he needed to catch the suspect, who was moving around town in a yellow Chevrolet, right away.

"There's something fishy going on here," Chele Pedro mumbled. "Pineda and the boys were in the middle of a very delicate investigation."

An officer told them that at that very moment, the Commissioner was pulling into the parking lot. They saw him climb the stairs in his immaculate suit, his eyes a little glassy with drink. He'd clearly come from some fancy dinner or reception.

"You two, in my office," he ordered. He had a fierce look in his eyes and he was scowling. Right away, before they'd even closed the door, he laid into Handal. How could that madman still be out killing people all over the place without having been arrested? And he'd better have a good explanation for the murders of the DICA agents! Didn't he realize they were the best agents trained by the gringos? And for what? To come back and be killed by a lunatic who was supposedly getting revenge over an affair he'd had with Agent Pineda's ex-wife three years ago! Did he think anybody was going to buy a story like that?

"It's the only story that makes sense, sir," Handal murmured.

The Commissioner had sat down behind his desk and was looking through a pile of folders. Handal and Chele Pedro were standing at attention.

"But there are still the murders of my niece, Mrs. Ferracuti and the rest of the boys from DICA!" the Commissioner screamed. "Is that not enough for you?"

Handal kept quiet. There was no use now in trying to explain to them that those deaths had been accidental.

Chele Pedro turned to look at him with a sarcastic expression that read: You're screwed.

"Tell him what they were up to, Pedro."

The DICA Chief explained that Agent Pineda's group was investigating the Cali cartel that operated throughout the country, not just in terms of drug trafficking, but they were also looking at investments and money laundering.

"The gringos are going to go apeshit," the Commissioner said. "They're going to want a good explanation, not the garbage you just gave us. Get me that son-of-a-bitch tonight!"

The Deputy Commissioner went down the staircase again. He was pissed off. Those two idiots didn't understand how much work he'd put in, but when he got that Bustillo they'd have to eat crow. Especially Chele Pedro. He could shove those sarcastic little looks right up his ass.

He told Villalta to move over, he'd drive. They left headquarters at top speed, tires screeching, the siren blaring as loud as it could go, as if they were on their way to a place where the yellow Chevrolet sat waiting for them. But they were only driving around with no real destination. They were getting closer to the bars, keeping in touch with the units they'd placed on surveillance, when Flores casually suggested they head for the Zona Rosa entertainment district – the best place to find the kind of crowds Bustillo liked to target.

"Of course!" Handal exclaimed.

He asked for backup cars to patrol the area before the suspect and his snakes could show up to cause a panic and end another dozen lives.

"Listen boss, he still might find a whole bunch of people on Los Mártires Boulevard," said Villalta while the Deputy Commissioner parked the Nissan by one of the intersections just before the Zona Rosa. Handal told him not to be an idiot. That was a main artery and there were crowds all up and down it, not concentrated in little areas, like at the supermarket or the gas station. But Bustillo hadn't ever repeated targets. Handal leaned back in his seat to get comfortable. This could be a long wait. Outside, a bunch of well-dressed kids were coming and going from bars and clubs, in little groups, drinking and smoking marijuana. They always made sure to stand as near as they could to the nicest car, the most expensive one, the least attainable.

"Looking at them makes you wonder whether it wouldn't be a good thing to have a few Jacinto Bustillos to get rid of all that stupidity," Handal murmured after a few minutes of silence, once his anger from the meeting with the Commissioner and Chele Pedro had diminished.

"Man to man, boss, what do you think happened to Bustillo?" Flores asked from the back seat.

It was getting cold. None of the units had reported any suspicious activity. Handal scratched inside his ear with his little finger and mumbled, "Maybe only Doña Sofía Pineda knows."

They were there until three in the morning, along with the other units who were searching all the streets that led to the Zona Rosa, a strategy that was supposed to lead Bustillo into a trap he couldn't escape from, but for whatever reason, that never happened. They decided to go back to headquarters and sleep, if only for a few hours, as long as Bustillo didn't decide to attack again at dawn. Their return was a little like defeat, and all of them wanted to forget about the case for a while. In a few hours, when the Black Palace was up and running on Saturday morning, they'd be exactly where they were now: with a great theory to explain the tragic events of the previous day, but still lacking the arrest that would be the mother of all proof.

Handal went up to his office, turned off the lights and leaned back in one of the armchairs. His instinct told him that was it for the day, that Bustillo and his snakes were dozing in the yellow Chevrolet, hidden in a garage somewhere. Maybe one right near the Black Palace.

At twenty after six the next morning the Deputy Commissioner made a few checks, but the suspect hadn't shown up anywhere. He called his wife to tell her that he'd be by in half an hour to shower, change and have a decent breakfast. They'd just brought him the newspapers. Now he'd really start feeling the pressure, he thought, even though Rita hadn't published anything about the link she suspected between the deaths of Sofía Bustillo and Agent Pineda.

But he didn't get out of the office. Chele Pedro called him to say he needed to talk to him; there were reports that could refocus the investigation. He'd better wait for him; he'd be there in half an hour at the latest. Other reports? That son-of-a-bitch was already trying to position himself to take charge of the investigation.

Flores and Villalta came in to ask for permission to take an hour to go home and shower. He told them to hurry. Chele Pedro was already trying to get them thrown off the case. There was no way those shits from DICA were collecting the medals for the work his team had spent all yesterday doing.

He took a shower, but put on the same clothes as the night before. He figured he'd get a quick breakfast at McDonald's or at Biggest. What the hell was Chele Pedro going to come up with?

Then the phone rang. The operator told him a man who refused to give his name had called to say that up to half an hour ago, the yellow Chevrolet had been parked at the Lomas del Guijaro, a new housing project still under construction, just a few kilometres away from Jardines de la Sabana, in the suburbs. Handal looked at his map of the city. If the anonymous tipster was telling the truth, Bustillo and his snakes were camping out near the city limits. Why the hell hadn't he thought of that? He ordered a unit to go search the area where, according to the tip, the yellow Chevrolet had spent the night. He backed away a little from the map, which covered a large part of the wall, after sticking red pins in the places Bustillo had struck or been seen. There wasn't any logic to it, or at least none that he could see. It seemed the suspect was picking his spots at random.

That's when Chele Pedro came in, solemn and with a stern look on his face. Pineda's group was investigating some bankers who were involved in laundering drug money, he said. He took a seat, rubbed his double chin without speaking and waited, as though this new revelation would suddenly enlighten Handal to the hidden motives behind the crimes. But the Deputy Commissioner, still standing, kept quiet and gave no sign that he understood.

"Mrs. Ferracuti," Chele Pedro finally muttered. "She was from a banking family . . ."

So now this idiot was trying to turn this case into a settling of scores by drug traffickers, without any proof, when that woman's death had been completely accidental, Handal thought. Just what he needed.

"Someone saw the yellow Chevrolet a little while ago," Handal said.

"Where?" Chele Pedro asked.

"In a new housing development called Lomas de Guijarro, near where he was operating last night."

"We have to get him," Chele Pedro replied as he walked out of the office, as if he were already in charge of the investigation.

The Deputy Commissioner sat back down in his swivel chair. He needed to eat something right away; his stomach was starting to burn. The phone rang. The operator said that someone wanted to talk to him directly to give him an urgent message.

"Put him on."

"The snakes just attacked Dr. Abraham Ferracuti's house," an anxious voice mumbled. "On the street that goes up to the volcano."

"What!" Handal exclaimed, jumping to his feet.

"I'm a neighbour. I saw the old yellow car they described in the newspaper go to the doctor's house. Then there were shots. Then the car left and headed up the street . . ."

THREE

Eight-twenty A.M.

Anxious, her curly hair still damp from the shower, Rita arrives at the newspaper office. She wears a flowing summer skirt and a sleeveless blouse.

Dr. Abraham Ferracuti has died.

She heard the news five minutes ago on the bus, when they interrupted the musical programming for a special news update.

She looks for Matías, the news editor, but he hasn't arrived yet.

El Zompopo hurries in with his camera dangling from his neck.

"I'm on my way over there right now," he says.

She asks him to wait a second, takes her tape recorder from her desk, grabs her walkie-talkie, and runs after him.

They get into the Volkswagen Beetle. Víctor, one of the newspaper's drivers, is at the wheel.

"Where are we going?" he asks.

"Towards the volcano, past Escandón," El Zompopo tells him.

Rita is in the back seat, chewing her nails. Ferracuti's death has just wrecked the angle she was working for her article for the Sunday supplement. She'll have to rethink it now. Shit!

"The snakes again," the driver says.

"But there were shots fired, too. There was a confrontation," El Zompopo answers.

Maybe one of those disgusting snakes died, she thinks to herself. She hates them. She doesn't know what she'd do if she ever saw one. Probably die of fright.

"Your pictures of the gas station came out great," she compliments El Zompopo, pointing at the newspaper she's leafing through. Last night, when she finally managed to get to the scene, the firefighters had nearly finished putting out the flames.

A helicopter flies over the slope of the volcano.

The street in front of Dr. Ferracuti's house is blocked off. There are police cars, the forensic unit's van, and luxury cars on the scene.

They hurry out of the Volkswagen. They pass police officers and bodyguards. An absent-minded officer asks to see their press passes, as if he doesn't know who they are.

El Zompopo takes pictures indiscriminately. The bodies are still fresh. Rita notices that the narcotics squad appears to be taking charge of the case. The DICA chief and his team of maniacs are moving around as if they're going to cordon off the crime scene.

Her colleagues from Radio Red, Sistema YSA and Canal 12 are there. Her competition from *El Gráfico* hasn't arrived yet. She looks around for Jonás and Arturo, the other two reporters assigned to the case by *Ocho Columnas*.

She walks over to Deputy Commissioner Handal. He's talking to Chele Pedro. Detective Flores stops her.

"The boss can't make any statements now."

Things are heating up.

The Police Commissioner himself comes through the front gate. She tries to approach him, tape recorder in hand, but his bodyguards stop her.

The Commissioner, Deputy Commissioner Handal, and Chele Pedro stand around Dr. Ferracuti's body, near the front door.

"He killed them all," Detective Villalta says in her ear. She flinches. She didn't see him coming.

Mirna and Epaminondas from *El Gráfico* arrive, followed by more colleagues.

"The wife, both girls, three maids, the security guard, the driver, and the bodyguards," Villalta whispers. "Ten in total, including the doctor. A total massacre."

The lead officers go into the house. The journalists have to wait outside, prowling around the bodies, the garage, and the garden, waiting to be let inside.

She looks at Dr. Ferracuti's body. A really good-looking man, she thinks, but the way he's laid out makes him look pathetic.

"It looks like they all died of snakebites," El Zompopo whispers to her.

"What about the shots?" she asks, turning to look at Villalta.

"The bodyguard emptied his submachine gun," the detective explains. "We think he was shooting at the yellow Chevrolet, because of all the glass on the ground. But there's no blood trail."

There's another commotion at the scene. The Minister of National Security himself has arrived: Dr. Ferracuti had been mentioned as a probable presidential candidate for the governing party.

The reporters swarm the minister, but the sour-faced cripple walks right into the house without stopping. Rita doesn't even try to get close to him. She's hated that conceited jerk ever since he publicly scolded her.

It looks like the yellow Chevrolet burst onto the property in a well-timed assault, Villalta explains to her. As soon as the security guard opened the automatic gate, the car ran him over and crashed into the Mercedes Benz to stop it. The security guard managed to react, but the snakes were quicker.

Rita's walkie-talkie squawks. It's Matías, the news editor, anxiously asking for details. She tells him that with the death of Ferracuti, the case has taken a new turn and they'll have to find a different angle for the story. He says the shit must have really hit the fan if the Minister felt obliged to come to the crime scene. He orders her to get back to the office right away.

She approaches Villalta again.

"So the stuff about Jacinto Bustillo is down the drain, right?" she asks, biting her nails.

He shrugs his shoulders.

El Zompopo sketches a diagram with the location of the bodies and the Mercedes Benz in his notepad so that the graphics guys won't complain that they don't have enough information.

The lead officers come out of the house.

The Minister steps forward and announces that the government will respond to this terrorism with the full force of the law against whoever perpetrated it; that Dr. Ferracuti was one of the most distinguished citizens in the country and that the President has ordered that a special committee be formed and led by the Police Commissioner to investigate the crimes committed by the snakes and the psychopaths who control them.

"Minister, was there an orchestrated plan, a conspiracy, behind these snake attacks?" asks Omar, the reporter from Radio Red, a young guy too interested in getting along with government officials for Rita's taste.

The Minister says it's still too early to make assumptions, but it wouldn't surprise him if certain suspicious groups were using an insane snake charmer for their own criminal ends. He heads towards the street, surrounded by bodyguards.

Rita confronts the Police Commissioner.

"Commissioner, why the Ferracuti family? Are the crimes related to the Doctor's possible nomination for the presidency?"

He can't reveal anything that may hinder the investigation, he answers, frowning. And reporters won't be allowed to go inside the home out of respect for the Ferracuti family, he adds.

"One of the daughters was naked," Villalta whispers to Rita, rubbing his jaw, a lustful look on his face.

Jonás and Arturo run over.

"We got lost," says Jonás. He's clumsy and skinny, and has a habit of stroking his moustache at the slightest provocation.

They've both been assigned to the story. They're covering the facts, the timeline and the background; she's writing the in-depth reports.

Handal and Chele Pedro follow the Commissioner out.

"Has Narcotics taken over the case?" she asks Villalta.

No, not at all. Didn't she just hear that they were going to form a special committee led by the Commissioner himself? It's even possible that staff from the State Intelligence Department, the President's own organization, will be involved in the investigation.

She has to get back to the office right away to talk to Matías and get organized. If not, it'll be impossible to structure her article. El Zompopo says he'll stay behind with Jonás and Arturo to wait and see if they can get inside the house.

Roger was right, she thinks, as she climbs into the Volkswagen. This is much more complicated than she'd thought, and now there are nationwide consequences. They argued about it last night after she'd come home from work, shaken by the events at the gas station and at Agent Raúl Pineda's house.

"What a bizarre massacre," Víctor, the driver says, as he adjusts the dial on the walkie-talkie. There's always interference in this part of the city.

Roger is her partner, a Frenchman in love with the tropics, with whom she's lived for six months. A leftist who can cook and fuck wonderfully, but who's stubborn and domineering, qualities he showed again last night when he went to bed angry that she refused to believe there could be political motives behind the snake attacks. "A destabilizing factor," he called it. Even that's possible now.

"They say the narcotics team murder is related to the doctor's death," Víctor says. He's one of those people who always seem to know what's going on, even though they don't write anything. "I've got a buddy in the department. He told me Pineda and his guys were investigating some bankers who were involved in money laundering," he adds.

"Were they investigating Ferracuti?" Rita asks, incredulous.

"No, Miss Rita, the doctor was collaborating with the investigation and his sister may have been, too. You know they were a banking family. That's what my buddy told me."

It's five after nine when she climbs the stairs to the office, anxious and getting tangled up in her summer skirt, her curly hair shining.

She walks by her desk and leaves the walkie-talkie and tape recorder there. Then she goes to the washroom. She always feels like she has to pee before a meeting with the news editor. She phones Roger right away, before she forgets, to tell him that with all the work she has to do, they'll have to skip lunch together.

Matías Cano is waiting for her in his office. He's fat and bald, with thick lips and little round glasses.

"There's an emergency cabinet meeting at the Presidential Palace. It's scheduled for eleven o'clock. Don't you tell anyone about it, all right? They've supposedly only leaked it to us."

He smokes and drinks coffee compulsively. His office reeks of tobacco. He's wearing a white guayabera shirt and dark pants.

Rita tells him the driver's story, that the murder of the DICA agents and the Ferracutis are connected.

"Could be," Matías says. "The way things are going now, we can't rule anything out."

He gets up and paces around the office. He goes back to his chair, takes a sip of coffee, looks at his computer screen, edits a paragraph, and suddenly turns back to Rita.

"Have you figured out the connection between the Bustillos and the DICA agents?"

She says her source has only confirmed that Jacinto Bustillo is the man in the yellow Chevrolet, but he refused to tell her why he attacked the narcotics agents.

"What's your angle?"

She'd like to wait until the early afternoon to discuss any angles, after the meeting at the Presidential Palace. For now, she can think of two possibilities: the first is a lunatic getting revenge on his wife and causing chaos all over the city while he's at it; the second, that the crimes were planned by a drug cartel to stop the investigation that threatened to expose their local financial advisors.

"But only Mrs. Bustillo was stabbed to death," Matías says. "That's important. It's the only crime. The snakes can't be tried for anything."

Rita feels an urgent need to pee again.

"You need to be here by two," he tells her, "so we can have one last meeting. I want this article by seven at the latest. Understood?"

It's always the same story. Early in the morning, you can't even smell Matías's breath, but late at night, by the time the office closes, his mouth is like a sewer.

She's about to leave when he says, "and don't forget the third possibility – an attempt to destabilize the government. The party moderates all agreed on Ferracuti."

The same stubborn theory as Roger's. Shit!

It's possible that Deputy Commissioner Handal and Chele Pedro are at odds on this case, she thinks while she runs to the washroom. But it's going to be hard to find sources willing to talk about Ferracuti. Upper-class people tend to run from reporters in these kinds of situations.

She goes back to her desk. She looks through her agenda. She wasn't able to get an interview with Mrs. Bustillo's daughter yesterday – a profile of her father would have been a major journalistic coup, even though the case is beginning to look political. She also needs to track down someone from Agent Raúl Pineda's family. They must have killed him at home for a reason.

She picks up the phone.

She asks to speak to Detective Villalta.

"It's his sister Mirna," she says.

He comes on the line.

"I need a big favour," she says. "I'm trying to find a relative of Agent Pineda's."

He suggests she call the DICA.

But those guys are a bunch of arrogant thugs, that's why she prefers dealing with Deputy Commissioner Handal and his people. He isn't so bad really, and sometimes he even gives her a few leads.

So Villalta says he's going to tell her something that would have been an absolute gift last night, but the way things are turning out, is probably less significant now than it had seemed: Pineda's wife, who was killed a few years ago, was Jacinto Bustillo's mistress.

He hangs up.

She stands, dazed, the receiver stuck to her ear. She runs to Matías's office.

"So where do the deaths of the Ferracutis fit in?" he mumbles, shocked by the news.

"There's got to be an explanation, a link somewhere," she says.

Yeah, that it's got nothing to do with drug trafficking or Ferracuti's possible candidacy, she thinks to herself. She says nothing because, like Roger, her boss is overly obsessed with politics. She tends to look for the human side of the story.

El Zompopo, Jonás and Arturo burst in.

"I got inside," El Zompopo says, grinning.

"It was gruesome," Jonás murmurs.

"And the pictures?"

The only one they wouldn't let him take was of the naked girl, El Zompopo explains, and brags that

Epaminondas, from *El Gráfico*, didn't even see him go in through the kitchen door.

Matías tells El Zompopo and Jonás to go find Conejo Arango, the government party President, and some opposition party leaders to get their reactions to Ferracuti's death. Arturo will go to police headquarters and report any strange goings-on.

Jonás strokes his moustache and turns to look at El Zompopo as if he isn't too sure about his new assignment, but Matías tells them to hurry up, what are they waiting for.

"Get down to the Presidential Palace right now," he tells her when the others have left the office, a cigarette jammed in the corner of his mouth. "It looks like they pushed up the meeting. And stay alert – the snakes could attack again."

Rita goes to her desk, puts on the navy blue jacket she always keeps on the back of her chair, and hurries to the parking lot. She'll find something out, even if it's just confirmation that the emergency cabinet meeting really is taking place and a list of who's there.

Víctor is waiting for her in the Volkswagen.

It's beginning to get warmer. She can feel a kind of tension in the air. There are fearful faces on street corners and at bus stops, as if people are expecting an old yellow car loaded with snakes to pull up any minute.

"All the big bosses are going to meet, right?" says Víctor, as though what goes on at the Presidential Palace were public knowledge.

"Who told you?" Rita asks.

"Everyone knows, Miss. I've got a buddy who works there. He says he wouldn't be surprised if they call a state of emergency. The president is really worried."

They arrive at the front gate.

The guard asks with whom she has an appointment.

She explains that she's here to ask Ms. Cuevas, the Assistant Press Secretary, some questions and shows him her press pass.

And then, when the guard opens the metal gate and Víctor begins to inch the Volkswagen forward, she spots a flash of yellow out of the corner of her eye. She turns around and sees an old American car drive by the Presidential Palace gates.

She screams so loudly, so hysterically, that Víctor nearly loses control of the Volkswagen.

"Miss, what's going on?" he manages to ask.

Her face is contorted with fear.

"The snakes!" she shouts. "They're coming!"

She runs out of the car.

"The Chevrolet with the snakes is out there!" she yells as she runs towards the building, growing more and more panicked.

A couple of security guards manage to stop her.

Alarmed employees come closer. Most of them know she's a reporter from *Ocho Columnas*.

They tell her to calm down, but Rita points to the front gate, still trembling.

"The car with the snakes just drove by! I saw it when we were coming inside! It's gone now but it's going to come back to attack us right here!"

Víctor, Ms. Cuevas, and the Chief of Security, Colonel Martínez, run over.

"I didn't see anything," Víctor says.

"Are you sure?" Colonel Martínez asks her, visibly alarmed.

"I'm covering the story for the newspaper," she says vehemently. "It was an old American car! What more do you want? Do something! The snakes will be here any minute!"

A heavy silence falls on the employees; terror begins to spread on their faces.

Colonel Martínez grabs his radio and shouts, "We've got a twenty-seven-five! Red alert! Lock all the doors and windows!"

Panic spreads. Everyone is talking at once, hoping the snakes won't make it inside. The worst thing right now would be an attack on the President. They ask God to protect them. Colonel Martínez orders them to stay calm, to go back to their work stations, and not to make any outside calls while they set up the defence mechanisms.

Ms. Cuevas takes Rita by the arm and walks her to her office.

"I never would have thought this could happen," the elegant and well-mannered civil servant murmurs.

Rita continues to tremble.

The Assistant Press Secretary offers her a glass of water and tells her to stay calm; nothing can happen to her here, security is airtight. Those reptiles will be burned to a crisp if they even try to get close.

She needs to call the office and speak to her boss, Rita stammers, a little calmer now. She tries to turn on her walkie-talkie, but all the frequencies have been jammed because of the red alert. She's in the Presidential Palace, the safest place in the country, Ms. Cuevas tells her. It's better if she doesn't try to use the telephone until this has all passed.

Colonel Martínez comes in looking for Rita.

"Come with me," he says.

They climb the stairs to the President's office.

And there they are, anxiously sitting around a rectangular table, their faces pale, as if the country were going through its worst disaster: the President, the Ministers of Defence and National Security, the Police Commissioner and the Chief of Intelligence.

"She's the witness, Mr. President," Colonel Martínez says.

The fat man's jowls are quivering, his tie undone and his sleeves rolled up.

"You saw him?" he wheezes.

"Yes, Mr. President," she mumbles. "I thought he was going to come up behind us while the gate was open like he did at Dr. Ferracuti's house, but he drove by, thank God."

The reference to Ferracuti impresses them.

General Morado, the Minister of Defence, says the helicopter is on its way to evacuate them from the area.

But the Presidential Palace is an old colonial mansion. The helicopter pad is on the lawn. The snakes could attack them while they're getting ready to climb aboard, warns Colonel Martínez.

They should set up a perimeter, suggests the sour-faced cripple Rita hates so much.

"Minister, do you think we can stop them with guns?" asks Colonel Martínez.

He said it without a trace of sarcasm, trying to think straight in his bewildered state.

General Morado says he needs a commando unit armed with flamethrowers – it's the only way to make sure the snakes are neutralized.

Colonel Martínez runs out, shouting the evacuation orders into his walkie-talkie.

Suddenly alone among the men who decide the country's fate, Rita realizes that she's right in the middle of the story, a privileged participant in the worst crisis the country has faced in years, the only witness. It's an experience that will raise her above her peers, provided the snakes don't kill her first.

The Police Commissioner informs them that his units are scouring the area and haven't yet found the yellow Chevrolet.

They can hear the helicopter approaching.

The snakes might be in the garden next to the helicopter pad, waiting for them, and they'll all go out only to get bitten, stammers the Chief of Intelligence, a chubby publicist who, according to Matías, got the job only because he manages the brothels owned by members of the top military brass.

Colonel Martínez bursts in to say the staff is hysterical. He asks for instructions.

Everyone is standing now, leaning out the window, watching the helicopter land.

General Morado tells Martínez to take the employees down to the basement where they'll be safe until the commando unit arrives to search the gardens.

"Mr. President, does this mean there really is a conspiracy to destabilize the government?" Rita asks before they take her downstairs with the employees.

"Miss," he says, rolling down his sleeves, "we're not about to make any statements to the press."

He makes a gesture to have her removed.

But when Colonel Martínez takes her by the arm to go down the stairs, they hear a burst of machine gun fire coming from the entrance of the building.

Dozens of employees race up the stairs. Several guards come up behind them walking backwards, their weapons pointed at the terrace.

"The snakes!" screams a panicked elderly secretary who's standing in front of the presidential office.

"What's happening?" asks Colonel Martínez.

"The troops are getting nervous, Colonel!" an official shouts from the ground floor. "A guard thought he saw a snake at the front gate and fired."

The Colonel lets go of Rita and goes down the stairs with his pistol drawn.

Ms. Cuevas asks her if the President is still in his office with the ministers. She says yes, they're waiting for a commando unit to escort them out.

"Oh God, I hope they haven't got in," says Víctor, who ran upstairs with the employees in all the confusion.

"Everyone go down to the basement!" the Colonel orders from the bottom of the staircase. "You'll be safe there while they search the gardens and evacuate the President!"

The staff members look at one another, fearful and indecisive.

"None of the snakes has got in! It was a false alarm!" shouts the colonel, trying to calm them down.

The office door opens, the Commissioner comes out and hurries down the stairs. Rita runs after him as if she's suddenly forgotten about the snakes.

"Who's responsible for this attack?"

But the President's entourage is following right behind them.

She moves to the side.

A Special Forces unit has split into two lines on the lawn for the President and his men to hurry between.

The helicopter's engine is on.

As soon as the cabinet ministers are aboard, it takes off.

Colonel Martínez leaves the lawn and orders the commando unit to comb the gardens.

Rita leans on the doorjamb. Surely the reptiles are coiled on some nearby garden path, but will they attack now that the president has left the building and a military commando unit armed with flamethrowers has taken up the search?

The employees have cautiously returned to the ground floor. Few of them go back to work, most are standing around the windows and the front entrance, curious and whispering, waiting for the slightest sign that they should run down to the basement.

Rita again tries to turn on her walkie-talkie, but the frequency is still jammed.

Víctor asks her what they should do now.

"Let's wait here a little while," she says, biting her nails.

Ms. Cuevas walks up beside her.

"Do you think they'll call a state of emergency?" Rita asks.

She doesn't know, this kind of situation is unheard-of; there are a ton of different accounts of what's happened and the president is extremely nervous. This crisis could paralyze the whole country.

The Special Forces unit has combed through even the most secluded parts of the gardens, and hasn't found any trace of the snakes. A calm begins to spread inside the building.

"I've got to get back to the office," Rita says, but she still doesn't feel brave enough to cross the lawn and head for the parking lot, even though the entire area is teeming with men in uniform armed with high-powered weapons.

She wonders why the Chevrolet didn't take the opportunity to follow her into the Presidential Palace. What stopped it? Maybe it was just a reconnaissance mission. She's in Ms. Cuevas's office now, drinking a Coke, thinking she won't write an article, but rather a first-person account of the events, a testimonial that'll make her colleagues drool with envy. A piece that will expose the effects of the snake attacks on the country's political leadership. Assistant Press Secretary Cuevas tells her to be cautious, moderate, and not to put the President in an awkward position. He's having enough trouble dealing with this crisis and doesn't deserve to have his image further damaged. Matías will disagree completely: he'll push her to write an article exposing the panic and chaos that's spreading so rapidly among the political leadership that the President doesn't even feel safe in the Presidential Palace.

She turns on the walkie-talkie. The frequency is clear. She tells Matías about spotting the yellow Chevrolet, about the chaos in the building, the cancellation of the emergency cabinet meeting, and the evacuation of the President and his ministers by helicopter.

"Do you know where they went?' Matías asks.

No idea. Maybe to Police Headquarters or the National Defence Building, she speculates.

He tells her to try and find out the President's whereabouts and get back to the office.

She leaves the Assistant Press Secretary's office and looks for Colonel Martínez. She finds him on the lawn, talking with two Special Forces lieutenants. The colonel claims not to know where the helicopter went.

Rita calls Víctor and tells him to bring the Volkswagen around. The search has been called off and they're authorized to leave the premises. They drive through the front gates at ten after eleven. There are groups of reporters outside waiting, proof that word of a possible snake attack at the Presidential Palace has filtered out to the city's news outlets. She waves to them without stopping. The heat outside is oppressive and sticky, as if there's an afternoon storm brewing. They drive in silence, exhausted by the morning's bizarre events, falling into the relaxed state that follows extreme stress.

"It's too bad there weren't any photographers there," she murmurs when they get to the office.

Her colleagues question her as she walks by, hungry for details, but before she can tell them anything, she has to report to Matías. She hangs her jacket over the back of her chair, takes a quick trip to the washroom, and goes into the boss's office.

Arturo sent the good news from Police Headquarters. They found the old, yellow, American car that drove past the Presidential Palace, but it was a Ford, not a Chevrolet, and the driver was a respectable engineer as terrified of snakes and reptiles as anyone else.

Rita falls back on a chair.

"It can't be," she says.

Matías's breath has gotten considerably worse, as if he's spent the last hour shoving coffee and cigarettes in his mouth.

"At least you created a story for yourself," he says. "Not all reporters can do that."

She lets out a nervous giggle and bites her nails. What will her colleagues think of her? What will the officials at the Presidential Palace say when they find out?

Matías tells her she's got two jobs to do: write an article as quickly as possible about the disturbance at the Presidential Palace, placing a special emphasis on how the President fled, then finish up her in-depth report.

Rita goes back to her desk, calls Roger to explain what happened and to tell him it'll be impossible for them to have dinner together. She turns on her computer and starts writing, just like that, with no outline. She already knows what she wants to say and if she stops to think about it, she might get stuck.

But she finds it impossible to write the article in first person, to confess how terrified she was after she saw the wrong yellow car, to explain the chaos she caused in the building. The two pages she's written scarcely explain the details of the President's evacuation.

She prints it out, rereads it and walks over to Matías's office.

"This is no good," he says, throwing the paper on the desk. He uses the butt of his cigarette to light another. "I asked you for a first-person account, something about your own experience, something with colour, something strong, not a press release."

Rita is standing in front of the desk. She feels an unbearable urge to pee.

"But I can't write that I caused all that commotion because I thought it was the car with the snakes," she stammers.

"Why not? That's what you have to write!" Matías shouts. "You say you were going inside to cover the emergency cabinet meeting when you saw an old yellow car. You told the chief of security and that's when the ruckus started! Stop pussyfooting around! This is garbage!" he says, pointing at the paper. "You didn't even need to be there to write that!"

She doesn't answer. Red-faced and gritting her teeth, she leaves. Who does that foul-breathed, bald-headed fool think he is, screaming at her like that? He wants to make her look ridiculous, to burn her, to get an exclusive at her expense.

She sits back down in front of the computer. She's hungry; she needs to put something in her stomach. She'll ask one of the couriers to get her a salad at the pizza place on the corner. Feverishly, almost furiously, she starts to formulate the story she'd like to write – not the one Matías is demanding, not the one Roger would dream up, but her own. An intimate story, the one she'd like to tell to herself in order to understand how, in twenty-four hours, life can suddenly take on a whole new meaning, and what you once thought was solid and secure can be exposed as incredibly vulnerable.

But the phone takes her out of her thoughts.

She lifts the receiver.

A rasping, nasal voice like that of an old drunk mumbles, "You don't know me, but you've written about me and I know you'd like to meet me. My name is Jacinto Bustillo, the driver of the yellow Chevrolet, a friend of the snakes, the one you thought you saw a few hours ago in front of the Presidential Palace. Don't talk, don't ask any questions, and don't interrupt me, because if you do, I'll hang up. I'll tell you what I have to say and that's it. Everything that's been written and said about me hasn't captured the essence, the real truth, of what's happening."

He pauses and sucks in a breath. He's smoking, Rita thinks to herself. She turns on her tape recorder and connects the microphone to the receiver.

118

"Your article this morning and the editorial took a shot in the dark. But I'm not crazy, and I'm not a criminal. I'm just someone who through tremendous effort and sheer will became what I am today: Jacinto Bustillo, the man with the snakes."

Another pause. Without letting go of the phone, Rita gestures to Jonás and El Zompopo, who just came into the office. She covers the mouthpiece and whispers that Jacinto Bustillo is on the line and to tell Matías to come quickly, before he hangs up.

"It must have been me you saw driving by the Presidential Palace," the voice continues. "But that's not important. I've been all over the city. If I didn't get inside the politicians' lair it's because I wasn't meant to."

Matías comes running, exhilarated. He tells her to ask Bustillo for an interview, anywhere he likes and on his conditions. She keeps her hand over the mouthpiece and explains that she can't interrupt him or he'll hang up. Matías orders the staff to be quiet, pushes the *loudness* button and then, in the middle of the tense, expectant atmosphere, they hear the voice calmly say, "There's no plan and there's no conspiracy, the way they're saying on the radio. Only chance and logic have allowed me to complete my mutation. But you wouldn't understand."

There's another pause, another drag on the cigarette.

"I'll call you back."

He hangs up.

They stand there open-mouthed for a few seconds. Then they all start talking at once, loudly and excitedly. A few wonder whether it could have been a hoax, others mention the tone of his voice; those who have just arrived scold Rita for not having been more aggressive.

Matías tells her to transcribe the recording right away and to bring him a copy as soon as it's ready.

"We've done it!" he exclaims, delighted. "With your account of what happened at the Presidential Palace and this transcript, we're going to blow them out of the water."

"What if he calls back?" Rita asks.

"Cut him off. Start talking to him. Make him trust you, tell him you do understand."

But she's not happy about having to transcribe the tape. She needs to finish her article and then start her in-depth report. Isn't that enough already?

Matías says fine, Jonás will write the transcript while she concentrates on writing a piece that needs a new dimension, now that Jacinto Bustillo himself has confessed that he and his snakes drove by the Presidential Palace and caused all the commotion that forced the President and his ministers to be evacuated.

That's why Rita is so pleased, sitting at her computer. Her distraught entry into the corridors of power wasn't the product of a hysterical young woman's terror of being attacked by a bunch of snakes, but an astute reaction that enabled her to save the President of the Republic and his Security Cabinet from a possible attack by Jacinto Bustillo's reptiles.

Now she can write freely and at length. She can describe in detail the politicians' panic and vent her emotions in the first person, without having to avoid mentioning her own cowardice, or even her initial fit of panic.

Minutes later the phone rings again.

The entire office goes still. All eyes expectantly turn to look at her.

She lets it ring a few more times.

She bites her nails.

Matías comes over, nervously chewing the filter of his cigarette.

"Pick it up! Don't let him get away!"

She lifts the receiver, a million questions in her mind, waiting to hear that same quiet voice, but the switchboard operator tells her it isn't the man with the snakes.

"Villalta," Rita says, relieved.

A collective jeer goes up around the room.

Matías goes back to his office.

"We know Bustillo called you," the detective says.

She assures him that he didn't say anything worthwhile.

They need the tape right away; it will help them enormously with the investigation. It's the first time the suspect has made any contact, and the forensic psychologists can use it to create a profile.

She doesn't have the tape. She's extremely busy writing an article about what happened at the Presidential Palace. He should talk to Matías; he's the only one who can turn it over to them. She'll transfer him right away, so Villalta can explain it to him.

The detective passes the receiver to his boss, Deputy Commissioner Handal. This is an official request now, and it would be out of place for Villalta to order the news editor of one of the biggest newspapers in the country to give up the tape.

It's a matter of national security, Handal explains so there can't be any doubt on the other end of the line. It's for the sake of the President himself. They have to hand over the Bustillo tape without delay.

But Matías knows how to play this game.

"Of course, Deputy Commissioner, I just need a written request and a letter from the Commissioner promising it will only be used for police purposes and won't be shared with any other news outlet."

Handal is probably in his swivel chair with his feet up on his desk, hating this insolent hack who has very little sympathy for the government and even less for the police. Meanwhile, Matías can barely contain his satisfied smirk. He feels like blowing smoke rings.

"We need to keep in close contact," Handal mumbles. "So we can trace the call if he phones again."

"He'll call back, Deputy Commissioner, I'm sure of it. He promised."

Handal tells him he'll send an officer over who'll contact police headquarters right away to tell them which line Bustillo is on.

"Yes, but under the same conditions. I want a promise from the Commissioner that nothing will be leaked to other papers," Matías warns him. "If you want to set up a sting operation from here, I want an exclusive."

Fifteen minutes later, while Rita is still feverishly working on her first-person account, an extremely personal piece which, according to Jonás and Arturo, is going to win her the Best Journalist of the Year Award, detective Villalta himself comes into the office. He's excited; his large jaw is clenched and it's as if his radio is burning in his hands. He knows that in a few minutes, he'll be in the home stretch of the hunt. He's like an old bloodhound flexing his muscles after sniffing out the scent of his prey.

He wants to explain the tactics he'd like Rita to follow when she gets the call to make sure they have enough time to trace it accurately and set up plans to surround the area and arrest him right away.

But Rita is too involved in her piece, glued to her monitor, typing frantically. She tells him to get lost and not interrupt or distract her; to wait until she's finished.

"But you need to be prepared," Villalta complains. "What if the phone rings right now?"

She's unimpressed. She tells him to either keep quiet or leave, they'll call him when they have Bustillo on the line. Does he think she's an idiot who doesn't know how to handle this?

All he wants is to follow Handal's instructions, which are a key part of the plans being laid all over the city to get Bustillo: the entire operation's success rests with her ability to keep him talking. Handal and Flores are at headquarters right now on red alert, in constant communication with units stationed near phone booths at strategic points across the city, particularly on the outskirts, because Handal has a gut feeling the yellow Chevrolet is out in the open, even though continuous helicopter searches have turned up nothing.

Minutes, hours, the entire afternoon goes by, and Bustillo still hasn't called.

In that time, Rita has finished her article, and gone into Matías's office brandishing her three pages, victorious. This time that bald-headed fool will have to congratulate her. She's eaten her salad while chatting with Villalta, who's feeling incredibly restless from the long wait. Now she's working on the in-depth report, making use of some of the comments Bustillo made on the phone (even though they'll print the entire transcript separately) to question the theories that the crimes are part of a conspiracy to destabilize the government, or are acts of retaliation by drug traffickers.

She's received several calls from colleagues who have been following the story, from girlfriends looking for gossip about the "vipers," and one from Roger. She told him that the arrest of the lunatic with the snakes is largely dependent on her, much to the disgust of Villalta.

And just as Handal predicted in the afternoon, Jacinto Bustillo waits until dark to call her back, when Rita's nerves are completely shot from waiting.

She gets the call at seven-oh-three. She's barely halfway through her article.

The murmurs start at the switchboard and grow like an enormous, threatening wave.

When her phone rings, everyone at the newspaper is shaking.

Villalta immediately contacts headquarters.

A loaded, airless silence falls over the editorial office.

Many reporters who already finished their assignments have stayed behind just for this moment.

After the fifth ring, she lifts the receiver.

Matías and Villalta are watching her tensely, as if they're afraid he'll hang up the phone at the first sign that something's up.

"Hello," she says, trying to control the tremor in her voice. The urge to pee and to bite her nails has gone.

"It's me again," says the voice, calm and mellow.

Her phone is programmed to record and it's on speaker so the entire staff can listen in.

"Don Jacinto, I'd like you to help me, I don't want to print anything that isn't true. Please, let me ask you a few questions." She's talking quickly, vehemently, not giving him a chance to cut in. "What's your real motive for these attacks? What do you mean when you say you're trying to complete your mutation? Could you clarify what you said about it being an act of sheer will that changed you into what you are today? Do you feel any remorse for what's happened and for the people who have died?"

He doesn't answer. It's as though Rita's barrage of questions has stunned him.

"Don Jacinto, I'd also like to know about your relationship to the snakes," she adds, staring at the paper she scrawled notes on while she was eating and Villalta was explaining how to keep a suspect on the line.

"Where and how did you get them? How many are there? What kind are they? Do they follow your commands or do they act on their own? Why didn't they bite your wife?"

"I told you not to ask me any questions," Bustillo mumbles distractedly. "I called you because I was surprised that your newspaper devoted so much space to the ladies' work. This is the first time you've talked about me, and you haven't even met me. But something tells me you aren't being honest with me."

He slams the phone down. The newspaper office erupts into chaos.

Villalta radios headquarters to see if they were able to trace the call. El Zompopo, Jonás and Rita will ride with him to cover the arrest; it's part of the deal the Deputy Commissioner made with the news editor.

Handal orders him to hurry to the southwest end of the city. All units are headed there, near San Mateo, where the Bustillos lived. A helicopter squad and a Special Forces unit armed with flamethrowers are also on their way.

Rita doesn't even turn off her computer; she nearly slips as she runs down the stairs. She gets in the Nissan just as Villalta is pulling out. She knows she'll have the full story now, but Jacinto Bustillo's final words to her play over and over in her head: "Something tells me you aren't being honest with me."

FOUR

I slept soundly, until noon, when heat, hunger and thirst woke me. I was sore from the beating I'd taken the night before, tired of all the commotion, and hungover. My body was just getting used to its new condition. The ladies weren't in the car; perhaps they'd used the broken windshield to get out and lie in the sun. They too were tired, and unafraid of being discovered in the middle of the scrapyard. I was surprised no employee had come by to ask about the yellow Chevrolet. We were lucky we hadn't been noticed. The caretaker at the gate was probably an illiterate who didn't follow the news. It was noon on a Saturday and the place was completely deserted. It was just for us, as we deserved.

I got out of the car to stretch. A harsh sun beat down on the empty grounds. I drank some water and found one of the bottles of rum I'd taken from Raúl Pineda's house.

I laid out some of the leftover upholstery next to the Chevrolet and lit a small fire, poured some water into one of Don Jacinto's empty tin cans, tossed in the pieces of Valentina's flesh and got ready to make a soup that would energize me. While I waited for the water to boil, I picked up the bottle of rum, took a long swig and started to limp around the scrapyard, curious to see whether I could find any escape routes. And then I saw the ladies: the three of them, looking like those schoolgirls you see lying together at the beach enjoying the sun and the stares of onlookers. They didn't notice me. I kept walking. I inspected the fence that surrounded the yard. The part that faced the street was made of grey brick, but the areas next to the empty lots on either side of the scrapyard were made of chain link and had several holes in them. The far side ended abruptly at a ravine with a stream at the bottom. The yard was the size of a city block. Dozens of cars were piled up haphazardly. On my way back to the Chevrolet I found a faucet. I turned it on and a small but steady stream of water came out. The soup still hadn't boiled. I walked back over to the ladies. I sat down on the ground, in a thin shadow cast by a stack of three car frames. I took another sip of rum.

"This is my last cigarette," I said.

I crumpled the pack into a ball and threw it as far as I could.

They were in another world, in a state of such total relaxation and enjoyment that neither I nor anyone else could reach them; so peaceful they seemed almost harmless. They were all so different; each had her own character, her own style, her own look. And yet they were so supportive of one another, so committed in their affection. I missed Valentina, the most beautiful and sensuous, the warmest of them. I started to feel the nostalgia and sadness of someone who remembers a loved one.

"I'm making a soup with Valentina's remains," I mumbled.

They continued to ignore me.

I took another sip of rum, went back to the car and took out Valentina's skin so it could dry in the sun. The soup was boiling now, but I wanted to wait for the meat to be ready. It had to be tender and delicious, worthy of a girl like her. And since I didn't have any seasoning, I looked for the bags of marijuana I'd taken from Raúl Pineda's table and emptied them into the soup.

Moving all that junk around, I found a small radio in a corner of the car, behind the empty cans. It worked perfectly, as if it had new batteries. I tuned in to a news update on the state of emergency that had been declared by the Presidential Palace because of an imminent snake attack. In the end, it turned out to be a false alarm caused by a yellow Ford whose driver had nothing to do with the perpetrator of the attacks destroying the city. The announcer said Rita Mena, a journalist with *Ocho Columnas*, was at the scene at the Presidential

Palace covering an emergency cabinet meeting, and reported that stress and tension were prevailing even at the highest levels of government. Other sources claimed it was the reporter herself who had raised the alarm when she saw the yellow car as she entered the Presidential Palace.

I leafed through the newspaper I'd bought that morning. Mena's article was in the national news section.

But now the announcer was saying that according to anonymous police sources close to the investigation, Jacinto Bustillo, the ex-husband of the woman killed yesterday afternoon, was the man suspected to be driving the yellow Chevrolet and planning the snake attacks. They'd finally identified me!

I stirred the soup, which was thickening nicely, and tried a piece of meat to see if it was tender. My succulent lunch would be ready in less than a half hour. I had another sip of rum and took out some of the bread that I'd taken from the supermarket yesterday afternoon.

The announcer reported that there was a rumour that government insiders believed the snake attacks could be part of a plan to destabilize the country's leadership, a theory that had legs, especially considering that the murder of Dr. Abraham Ferracuti would intensify the infighting within the party. He also reported that a special committee had been formed, by presidential decree, to be led by the city's police commissioner to stop the snake attacks as soon as possible.

The news update ended. I turned the dial and found the classical music I needed to organize my thoughts. I lay down inside the car, the little radio resting on my abdomen, my hands laced at the back of my neck, and my gaze fixed on the rusty ceiling of the Chevrolet. They must have been looking desperately for us, with their entire arsenal, street by street, combing through parking lots and garages, ordered to annihilate us the instant we were spotted. My sore body was begging for rest and I nearly fell asleep, but hunger prevailed.

The soup was delicious and invigorating, the mix of snake meat and marijuana totally innovative. What a way to enjoy Valentina – it was as though every piece of meat had been infused with her voluptuousness, as though her capacity for extreme anger and pleasure was transmitted to me with every bite, as though her lustful spirit had been distilled in the thick, hot liquid. I remembered the dream I'd had the night before, when Valentina had wrapped herself around me in a slippery, orgasmic embrace, and the soup seemed to taste even better.

Once sated, instead of falling victim to the drowsiness that comes after a feast, I felt incredibly energized and lucid. I wanted to talk, to do something. But first I had to get cigarettes. I put out the fire, had a last sip of rum, tore out the page of the newspaper with the office's telephone numbers, and walked over to the scrapyard's front gate. I thought it would be bolted by now, that the yard would be completely abandoned during the weekend, and that the watchman would be gone. I was right. I looked for a hole in the chain link that I could go through to get to the vacant lot next to the yard. I made it to the sidewalk. I walked a few blocks, under the blazing sun, until I found a store.

Two young men were sitting on the steps with a trail of beers before them, hangovers still written all over their faces. They looked at me distrustfully. An elderly woman gave me the cigarettes without hiding her disgust. I felt like having a cold beer. I asked for one. I sat down on the steps. The soup had been marvellous and I felt sociable and animated. The young men became uncomfortable and guarded. They moved over to the other side of the steps. I lit a cigarette and offered them one. They said no thanks. I was so thirsty I drank half the bottle of beer in one gulp.

"Is there a phone booth around here?" I asked.

They told me it was three blocks away. I wondered whether they recognized my face from the composite sketch that was in the paper.

"I heard they caught that nut with the snakes," I said.

How? Where?

The old woman listened in from behind the counter.

"They just said it on the radio," I explained. "He went back downtown and they caught him there."

"I hope they kill that son-of-a-bitch," the clean-shaven one said angrily. Then he told me he'd like a cigarette after all.

"What are you talking about? It's too bad they caught him," said the one wearing sunglasses. "He had those politicians by the balls."

"I wonder if you'd like it if those snakes bit you or someone in your family."

The old woman said she was sure the appearance of the snakes was an ominous sign, evidence that the end of days was near, just like it said in Revelations. There was no other way to explain such a disaster.

I told them I agreed.

I drank the rest of my beer. I got up and limped off to find the telephone, remembering that I hadn't warned the ladies I'd be gone for a while.

I dialled one of the numbers listed for the newspaper office. I asked for Rita Mena. She came on the line quickly. I identified myself, warned her not to interrupt me or I'd hang up, and I told her everything that had been written about me hadn't captured the essence of what was happening.

"I'm not crazy, and I'm not a criminal. I'm just someone who through tremendous effort and sheer will became what I am today: Jacinto Bustillo, the man with the snakes," I said, inspired.

The poor girl was stunned. She kept quiet while I smoked.

I told her that it was me she'd seen driving by the Presidential Palace. But that didn't matter; I wasn't interested in getting inside the politicians' lair.

"There's no plan and there's no conspiracy, the way they're saying on the radio. Only chance and logic have allowed me to complete my mutation. But you wouldn't understand," I said, thrilled, as though I was able to express myself perfectly and freely for the very first time.

Before I hung up, I promised to call again.

I tossed my cigarette butt in the street. I walked back to the scrapyard, excited, wanting to see the ladies and tell them about the commotion we'd caused throughout the country so they could relish their fame, the fact that they were the talk of the town. But I didn't want to pass by the store again. I went down a parallel street and walked until I got to the vacant lot, where I turned to go back in the way I'd left.

The ladies had gone back to the Chevrolet. They'd had enough sun and were full of energy, as well as a hunger and thirst that had led them to finish the rest of the soup and Valentina's flesh. They were resting inside the car, looking placid and satisfied, which made me wonder what effect the mix of marijuana and Valentina would have on them.

I told them I'd gone to speak to one of the journalists who were writing about us. The whole city was in a panic. People thought they saw us and were afraid of being attacked in places we'd never been; crazy rumours about why we were attacking were spreading everywhere. It was as though we were the harbingers of political groups or drug traffickers trying to take power.

They looked at me silently and without changing their expressions, uninterested in my worries. I told them the authorities had identified me as Jacinto Bustillo, that they had a description of the yellow Chevrolet and were probably looking for us right now, determined to exterminate us as soon as the opportunity presented itself. That didn't impress them either. Rather, I noticed a certain gleam in their eyes and a hint of a smile that gave me the impression I should change tracks.

"I found a radio," I said, pointing to the set a little nervously. It was the first time I found myself unable to read their behaviour.

"We forgot to tell you," Beti said.

Don Jacinto listened to it every night, very quietly, so people walking by wouldn't notice that the car was being lived in, she added.

"He liked to listen to classical music to fall asleep," Carmela mumbled.

I turned on the radio. I tucked myself into a corner of the car, and stared at the set so I wouldn't have to look at them. I turned the dial until I found a rock music station called La Nueva Era. I felt a strange tingling that made me more and more nervous and restless. It got so strong I had to get out of the car. I lit a cigarette. I walked through the stacks of cars towards the fence at the back of the yard, feeling inexplicably uneasy, until I realized that the tingling was coming from my groin. Even worse, for a little while now I'd had a budding erection.

Goddamn! Then I understood. Valentina . . .

I took a walk around the scrapyard, downcast and smoking anxiously. My palms were damp with sweat. Although I was prolonging the minutes as much as I could, although I was getting the idea that this decision was only up to me, the moment would come, inevitable and precise, perhaps with a certain air of sarcasm, and it would do me no good to try and slap it or scare it away. On the contrary, I needed to drain it of its meatiest emotions, to discard my image as a sacrificial lamb and transform into one of an ephebe drunk with pleasure and lust.

I went back to the yellow Chevrolet. I got inside. They were as I'd left them, splendid in their peacefulness, a touch of mischief in their expressions. The radio was playing that song by Maná that went, "*No sabes cómo te deseo, no sabes cómo te he soñado.*"[1] I looked in my pockets.

"I want you to try something," I said.

"*Contigo yo alucinaría . . .*"[2]

---

1 "You don't know how much I want you, you don't know how much I've dreamed of you."

2 "You hypnotize me . . ."

I took out one of the bags of cocaine I'd taken from Raúl Pineda's table. I turned a can upside-down so I could use it as a flat surface and spread out the glittering white powder. Curious, they came closer.

"What is that?" Beti asked.

"Magic powder," I said. Then I spread some on my middle finger and offered it to her. "Try it. You'll like it."

She narrowed her eyes distrustfully at me.

"Don't be afraid."

She passed her forked tongue over my finger over and over again, until she finished the line.

"Now it's your turn," I said to Loli, the timid one, the most affectionate.

She turned to look at Beti, waiting for a reaction.

"Oye mi amor, no me digas que no . . ."[3]

I spread more cocaine on my finger and held it out to her. She licked it, as distrustful as Beti at first, but later with delight.

Carmela said she didn't want any; she wasn't about to go around experimenting. The soup had tired her out too much to try any unknown substances, what with the herbs I'd added to it.

"My tongue and mouth are asleep," said Beti. "But I'm starting to feel really good." Loli said the same thing was happening to her.

-----

3   "Listen, my love, don't say no . . ."

"Cheer up," I said to Carmela, the most obstinate one, the least tame. I brought my finger closer.

"*Oye mi amor, no me digas que no . . .*"

She frowned and licked my finger as if she were being forced.

I rolled up one of the letters Aurora had sent Don Jacinto and inhaled through it the pure, potent powder I'd taken from the narcotics officer.

"I want more," Beti said.

Loli said she did, too. She felt amazing, happy.

I gave them another round.

I did another two lines, while Carmela watched, still reluctant. But when Beti and Loli were finishing off their fourth dose, she said she wanted some too, before all that magic powder disappeared. She felt a delicious tickling below her belly, she said. She felt like doing you-know-what. The three of them looked at one another like accomplices, with that gleam in their eyes and that hint of a smile that had made me so nervous earlier.

The song had ended and some idiot was talking non-sense into the microphone. I turned the radio off.

"What's up?" I said.

I lolled back in the corner.

"That powder really turned me on," Beti said. She raised her plump body.

There was barely any coke left.

The tickling in my groin suddenly came back, but more intensely this time, and my growing erection was

140

starting to feel uncomfortably tight in my underwear. I took off all of my clothes. And, before I lay down on the blanket in the corner, I looked for the bottle of rum to see if there was any left. Beti was in front of me now, her head raised and her gaze beginning to drift away. I took a sip just as she started to slide over my thighs. She went past my erection and up my chest, slowly spreading herself along my skin. She rubbed her head into my neck, under my ear, while she excitedly stroked my penis and testicles with her lower body.

"That's nice," she murmured.

She coiled up the lower half of her body and wrapped it around my penis, gripping tightly, making circular movements. I caressed her head with my left hand and slid my right over the part she'd curved around my erection.

I moved over so she could lie on the car floor. Her body was stretched all the way out. I started to lick her all over her body, first her chest, then her belly, then all the way to the end of her tail. She'd never felt like this, she sighed. I got down on all fours so I could lick her better. That's when Carmela, the impulsive one with the short, thin body suddenly coiled herself around my erection and clung to it like a limpet. Without loosening her grip, she moved back and forth along my glans, getting me so excited I fell to the floor, begging them to stop for a minute and let me go, or I would come right then. I held my breath to try and stop the spasms. A few drops of semen leaked out of my throbbing penis.

Beti was stretched out, recovering. Carmela had moved over to the side, gasping for air. She was a very emotional girl.

Loli was the only one who kept still. She looked so long and thin with her neck lifted up, a shy expression on her delicate face. I looked her in the eyes. She held my gaze. She was the one I liked the most, no doubt about it. Something moved inside my chest when I looked at her. She was the only one I could fall in love with.

I went over to the can to finish the last bit of cocaine. I did a line and held out my finger to the little gluttons who kept asking for more.

I looked at Loli again.

"I want you," I said.

She looked down.

"Me too," she whispered. "But I'd like you to put some music on."

I picked up the radio.

"I want to dance with you," she said.

I told her the ceiling was too low; that I couldn't dance unless I did it on my knees.

"Let's get out," she said.

I got out, naked and anxious, my erection less hard. I put the radio on the ground and found a song by the Beatles called *Dear Prudence*. The sun was still blazing, even though it was much lower in the sky. She moved up my body and rested her head on my shoulder, her tail softly coiled around my penis. I put my hands on her back. I kissed her neck tenderly. Our connection was so intense it was as though the movements I made with my lips were being transferred directly to my penis. We moved softly and slowly, rhythmically, like two partners performing an ancient ritual.

"I could really fall in love with you," I whispered.

"Me too," she said, gripping my erection with her slippery skin. "I'd love to dance with you all afternoon."

The song ended.

Beti and Carmela had climbed up onto the hood of the Chevrolet and started banging on it with their tails, applauding us.

"That's lovely!" Beti exclaimed. "I want to dance, too."

Carmela suggested I dance one song with each of them. It was a beautiful afternoon and we had the whole scrapyard to ourselves.

Loli let go of me and climbed up to the hood looking a little saddened, I thought. We'd been too obvious and the others must have noticed that there was something more between us than just desire. Beti came over to me so we could dance to the next song that idiot DJ would play, as soon as he shut his mouth.

"That's nice," she said again.

I had to plant my feet firmly on the ground because she made a move that enabled her to stroke my penis, testicles and anus at once, in a kind of salacious merry-go-round. The dizziness that came over me was so strong and so sudden that I had to lean back on the car. That old Eric Clapton song *Layla* came on, and Beti moved up my body and laid her head on my shoulder.

"Did you like that?" she asked.

"Of course," I said, while we moved to the lively rhythm of Clapton's song. "I've never felt anything like it."

But something was off; there was a kind of discomfort, a growing distance between us, caused by the fact that I'd already chosen a girl who was watching a little sadly from the hood while I gorged myself with her friend. That didn't keep me from staying excited or my body from shaking at Beti's carnal touch, of course.

The song ended.

"It's my turn," Carmela said.

But you couldn't hold someone close and dance to the next song; it was the kind you had to sort of bop around to, or at least that's what I thought. I said so, without wanting to upset Carmela. I started to move to the rhythm of the Police song, singing along to the chorus, *Walking on the Moon*, while she sat upright in front of me, balancing herself and humming more and more enthusiastically, bordering on ecstasy, as though we really were walking on the moon, dancing between the craters. And then right before the song ended, I made out the sound of a helicopter that was flying low and getting closer.

Suddenly, a light went on in my head.

I shouted for them to get inside the Chevrolet.

I took out the blanket from inside the car as fast as I could and put it on the roof. I started frantically throwing dirt, ashes from the fire, and trash on the hood and the trunk, trying to camouflage the telltale yellow. Terrified, they'd gone inside to hide in those corners of the car where even I couldn't see them. I continued to camouflage the car until I thought the helicopter was almost directly over me and then I threw myself inside and slammed the door. I curled up in the middle, waiting for the worst – for the helicopter to land on the yellow Chevrolet and for the machine-gun fire, the explosions and the fire from the flamethrowers to start. The helicopter flew in low circles around the scrapyard looking for us among the hundreds of cars, stopped in mid-air a few times, once very close to the Chevrolet, and suddenly flew off.

I stayed frozen for several minutes, even after the sound of the helicopter had faded and I heard the radio I'd left on. Had they spotted us? Was their leaving just a strategy to get us to relax so they could launch a surprise attack?

I sat up. My heart was pounding. I needed a drink. I searched fruitlessly in every corner. The alcohol reserves had been finished off. But I did find another bag of cocaine, though a little smaller – Raúl Pineda had been very obliging. I cut myself some lines while the ladies came out of their hiding places.

"What was that?" Beti asked.

"They're looking for us," I said. "They want to kill us."

"I'm scared," Loli said.

I picked up Aurora's rolled-up letter to Don Jacinto and took a huge line. They begged to have some magic powder. They said the fright had left them completely crushed. I gave them enough to make Beti ask me to bring in the radio a few minutes later, so we could keep dancing, even if I had to do it on my knees inside the car. It was Jim Morrison's powerful, twanging voice singing *Riders on the Storm* that calmed me and restored my energy, and later my happiness at being with them, at having Loli by my side. The three of them had that gleam in their eyes and that suggestive expression again. I was still naked, sitting on the car floor. The helicopter had taken away my erection and my desire to dance, and the last line of coke had only intensified my thirst for alcohol. I picked up my underwear, my shirt and my pants.

"What are you doing?" Beti asked.

"I'm getting dressed."

"Why?" Loli asked a little sadly, as if she were trying to win me over.

I didn't know how to answer her.

"But I still want you," she whispered pleadingly.

I asked her to come closer. I took her by the head, face to face, and stared deep into her bright, unfathomable eyes. I kissed her on the mouth. She wasn't expecting it. She coiled herself around my neck and torso, completely overjoyed, and slid down to rub herself against my penis, intensely and outrageously. Beti and Carmela couldn't stand it either. They climbed on top of me so decisively and with such voracity that I had no choice but to let myself fall flat on my back, my arms open wide, while they began their lascivious feast between my pubic bone and my crotch – a feverish snake dance that quickly brought me to climax, spasms, howls and a gush of semen.

I was exhausted, but my heart was pounding as if it would never go back to normal. I rested a while, nearly falling asleep. I sat up slowly. I lit a cigarette. I got dressed without their objections because they were dozing softly. I desperately needed something to drink, even if it was just a case of beer. I got out of the car. Soon dusk would be upon us, with its orange light. I walked over to the vacant lot to go out to the street. But I felt a sudden urge to shit. I decided it would be better to go over by the fence at the back of the scrapyard, the one next to the ravine. I was curled up and distracted, enjoying the act of defecation, when I felt a presence behind me. I turned around. It was Loli. She slithered calmly towards me. I was embarrassed that she'd seen me like that.

"That was lovely," she said.

I agreed.

I wiped myself with Don Jacinto's letter. I pulled up my pants and looked for a hole in the chain link. We got out next to the ravine. The stream ran about thirty metres below. People swarmed around their hovels in a slum on the other side. I sat down on the very edge of the ravine, looking down into the emptiness, with her by my side.

"Do you think the helicopter will come back?" she asked.

Probably. The hunt had just begun and they weren't going to give up until they got us.

And what would we do if they cornered us in the scrapyard?

"Try to escape," I said.

It was as though the clouds had been painted with orange and pink brushstrokes. A cool, nighttime breeze blew over our side of the ravine.

"I think we'll be all right until Monday morning," I mumbled.

I threw a rock into the ravine.

"I love you," she said. "I want to be with you. I don't want anything to come between us."

I kept quiet, my gaze lost on the horizon. I put my hand on her back and caressed her tenderly.

"I love you, too," I finally said. "But I need a drink right now."

I stood up.

We went back to the scrapyard.

"I'm going to the store," I said. "Stay alert. There must be a whole bunch of creatures like you hiding between all these cars and I don't want you to get a nasty surprise."

"Be careful," she said and blew me a kiss.

I went back to the hole in the fence next to the vacant lot. I walked out to the street. The revelry was in full swing at the store; there were several groups of people drinking on the sidewalk. I tried to pass unnoticed, but a number of people looked over at me disgustedly. The two young men from the afternoon were still drinking. I asked for half a bottle of rum. I had just enough money left to cover it. The old woman recognized me from behind the counter.

"It was a lie," she snapped. "They haven't got those snakes yet."

The people near the entrance went quiet and turned to look at me.

"The journalist must have got it wrong," I said to the old woman. "There have been so many false alarms."

"I just heard that the snakes tried to attack the funeral home where they're showing Dr. Ferracuti and his family's remains," she said.

"I don't believe it," I exclaimed.

I opened the bottle and took a drink right there in the store.

"It's true," the old woman insisted. "It happened about an hour ago. He had to escape with his snakes because the police who were guarding the place surprised him."

The drink made me feel wonderful.

One of the people drinking said the President was going to give a public address at eight o'clock that night.

"They scared that fat bastard," another drinker said gleefully, referring to the President.

They guffawed and toasted one other.

I came over to them.

The clean-shaven young guy who had said he hoped they'd kill the man with the snakes that afternoon came to join us, swaying, completely drunk.

"This goddamn bum has gotta be Jacinto Bustillo," he mumbled, slapping me hard on the back.

Everyone cheered.

I started to perk up.

"If I were him, you'd have to be careful," I warned jokingly. "Because the snakes would get you, even in your dreams."

There was a burst of laughter, whistles and jeers.

The clean-shaven guy didn't find it funny, but caught something in my look that made him go back to where he'd come from, telling me to take my stink somewhere else.

"Don't listen to him, man," said the guy who'd made fun of the President. "You have your drink in peace. You know what? I'll buy you a beer. Niña Tila," he shouted, raising his arm towards the old woman, "a beer for the gentleman, please. If you were the guy who's screwing with those rich assholes and those piece-of-shit politicians, I'd carry you out of here on my shoulders."

There were more cheers and whistles.

I took the beer.

Everyone was talking about the same thing: the chaos caused by the snakes in the Chevrolet.

The guy with the sunglasses yelled over from another group of drinkers that we should start a committee to "show solidarity with Jacinto Bustillo and his avenging snakes," and that I, as head of all the bums in the city, should start an underground support network for Bustillo and his snakes.

We nearly pissed ourselves laughing.

But it was starting to get dark and I remembered that the ladies were all alone, waiting for me, especially Loli, who could get quite anxious.

I finished my beer, said thanks, told them I'd be back in a little while, and left. I limped over to the phone booth, my pocketknife with the bone-coloured handle rubbing against my thigh. I wondered whether it was worth it to call Rita Mena back to explain something to her that I wasn't even clear about. She'd probably already contacted the police and Deputy Commissioner Handal had probably had her phone line tapped, just like on television, waiting for my call so he could sic his hounds on my ladies and my poor bones.

I sat down on the curb next to the telephone. A teenage girl with meaty calves had the receiver stuck to her ear, laughing. I took another sip from my bottle, lit a cigarette and listened to her conversation. A little fat guy with a kind face lined up behind the girl.

"I'm next," I warned him so he wouldn't cut in line.

The fat guy said yes, of course. Nothing short of courteous.

Now the girl was talking about a friend from school named Gerardo who'd died last night during the snake attack at the Esso station.

I shamelessly looked at the dark hair on her fleshy calves. She looked uncomfortable and turned her back to me. The fat guy smiled at her.

"Listen, I'll call you later," she said. "There's a bunch of people waiting for the phone."

She hung up and crossed the street.

I got up slowly. The fat guy moved back a bit to get away from my stink. I took out the clipping with the newspaper office's phone number and dialled.

I asked to speak to Rita Mena.

The operator asked me who was calling, but there was a trembling in her voice that made me think she already knew, and was waiting to raise the alarm.

I said I was a friend, that it was personal.

She let her phone ring five times, as if she were waiting for them to be able to trace the call.

I turned to look at the fat guy and smiled.

"It's me again," I said.

But she didn't let me continue. She started asking a million questions, trying to confuse me and stall for time, like a real cop. I put my hand in my pocket and stroked the bone-coloured handle of my pocketknife.

"I told you not to ask me any questions," I said when she needed to take a breath. "I called you because I was surprised that your newspaper devoted so much space to the ladies' work. This is the first time you've talked about me, and you haven't even met me. But something tells me you aren't being honest with me."

I hung up, because I sensed my time was running out.

I said goodbye to the fat guy, who immediately grabbed the phone. I walked normally for about five metres and then started to run along the street parallel to the store, as fast as I could, as if I'd never had a limp, as if I'd never been Jacinto Bustillo.

I hadn't yet reached the vacant lot when the whirring of the helicopter blades and wailing of the sirens began to shake the neighbourhood.

The shots were terrible, heavy, very powerful. I pictured the terrified look on the fat man's face, destroyed by the impact without even knowing what was going on. I went into the vacant lot, crossed the fence, and ran to the yellow Chevrolet.

The din had already alerted the ladies.

"Quick!" I shouted. "Go out by the ravine!"

They hurried out. Loli turned around as if she were going to wait for me.

"Hurry!" I yelled in the midst of the deafening noise and the searchlights that danced wildly from the sky.

I ran after them and, before I made it to the ravine, a light nearly hit my back.

Everything happened in an instant – the shots, the flames, the explosions.

I slid through the hole in the chain-link fence and fell, tumbling down the ravine below. I landed in the filthy stream, completely dazed and worn out.

I had to get up right away, before another searchlight spotted me, before the tracer bullets combed the area.

The din from above was terrifying. The explosions lit up the sky so it looked like daytime.

I managed to sit up. I left in the direction of the stream, hidden on the shore, grabbing onto bushes, moving forward with great difficulty.

I couldn't see the ladies anywhere. I didn't even know if they'd fallen all the way down to the stream.

"Loli!" I screamed, but there was no answer.

I continued to wade through the ford until I found a path covered with enough vegetation for me to risk it.

The police were setting cars on fire indiscriminately. It was the only explanation for the thundering noise and the blaze. The helicopters were still in position, flying low and lighting up the scrapyard, the vacant lot, and the ravine.

I reached the edge of the slum. I passed through the outskirts, trying to avoid the people staring stupefied at the assault on the scrapyard. I took a dirt road that led to a busy street. I staggered around as if I were completely drunk to throw off the people worriedly going back to their homes, trying to get away from the kind of racket they hadn't heard since the grim days of the war.

I stumbled along, talking to myself, gesturing at the night, babbling. I called out to Loli. My love, my beautiful girl, come with me. I called out to Beti and Carmela, my princesses who had loved me so. Don't leave me, my darlings, what will I do without you, where have you gone? An hour later, exhausted, craving a drink, and weepy because I thought I'd never see them again, I spotted Niña's Beatriz's store. It was still open. I saw the spot where Don Jacinto's yellow Chevrolet had been parked with the ladies inside. It made me think about coincidences, because three days ago at the same hour, I'd approached the beggar walking back to his car, and at this time just two days ago, thanks to my pocketknife with the bone-coloured handle, I had turned into the filthy old snake charmer.

I climbed the staircase, took out my keys and opened the door to my sister Adriana's apartment.

155

"It's me," I said.

Adriana jumped off the couch to kiss me, crying and pestering me with questions: what happened to me, where had I been, how did I end up in such a sorry state? Damián was also happy I'd returned.

I said I needed to take a shower, shave, and change before I told them anything. I went into the bathroom. She called Deputy Commissioner Handal to tell him I'd come home, but he was away at the moment, extremely busy looking over the rubble of a scrapyard where Jacinto Bustillo, the snakes, and the yellow Chevrolet had been burned to ashes by flamethrowers and incendiary bombs.

San Pedro de los Pinos, D.F.,
September-October, 1995.

Translator's Acknowledgements

I would like to thank Marjorie Ratcliffe, Rafael Montano, Hugh Hazelton, Stephen Henighan, Christopher Bavota, my friends and family, and above all, Horacio Castellanos Moya.

About the Author

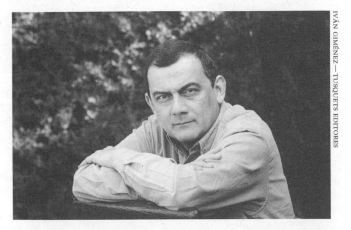

Horacio Castellanos Moya was born in 1957 in Honduras, but grew up in El Salvador. He has lived in Guatemala, Canada, Costa Rica, Mexico, Spain and Germany. His work has been translated into German, French, Italian, and Portuguese. His novel *Senselessness* was published in English to universal critical acclaim in 2008 by New Directions. He has published eight novels and is now living in exile as part of the City of Asylum project in Pittsburgh, Pennsylvania.

About the Translator

Lee Paula Springer works as a freelance translator and copy editor. She lives in Montreal. Her website is www.leepaula springer.com